10 JAN 2007

DEAD AGAINST THE LAWYERS

Radwick Holter was a successful QC, envied for his success and for Charlotte, his beautiful wife much younger than himself. One morning he finds an unpopular solicitor dead in his own office, the door to his collection of macabre murder weapons open, and a trail of blood.

On trial for this murder, Holter must conduct his own defence—will he be successful?

DEAD AGAINST THE LAWYERS

Roderic Jeffries

·BLACK·
DAGGER
·CRIME·

First published 1965
by
William Collins Sons & Co. Ltd.

This edition 2003 by Chivers Press
published by arrangement with
the author

ISBN 0 7540 8634 8

Copyright © 1965 by Roderic Jeffries

British Library Cataloguing in Publication Data available

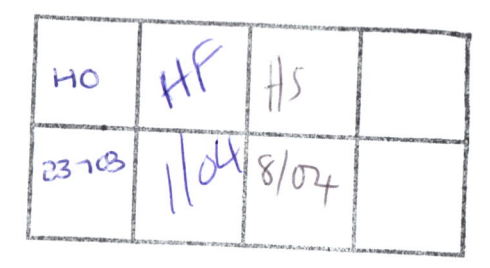

Printed and bound in Great Britain by Antony Rowe Ltd.,
Chippenham, Wiltshire

DEAD AGAINST THE LAWYERS

Chapter One

THE PRIVATE room in The Three Bells was decorated in common English provincial style: the wall-paper tried to look like oak panelling, the electric lights were in the form of candles, the unlit electric fire had canvas coals and electric flame shadows, the Persian carpet had been made in lower Manchester, and the lace tablecloth was plastic.

Mr Justice Thwaites stared at his glass of port as if that, too, was ersatz.

'Judge,' said Radwick Holter, 'this is an honour we hope will soon be repeated.'

The judge made no comment.

'It's far too long since the Hertonhurst Bar had the pleasure of dining the circuit judge.'

'Eight years and three months.'

'In this day and age of change, some of us are deeply concerned with the hard fight to preserve from the past all that's good. Your visit here, Judge, helps us – the smallest Bar and bar mess in the country – to preserve our identity and wage successfully that fight.'

Holter never knew when to stop talking, thought the judge. It was a trait that irritated the Bench but quite often seemed to impress both juries and clients. It was odd how the layman confused unnecessary rhetoric with telling advocacy and so preferred perorations to precision.

As Holter signalled to the waiter to hand round the cigars, he thought how clearly it was time the judge retired. For more than twenty years, now, his thin, sarcastic face had, in court, peered out from beneath a slate coloured wig as he dispensed justice with little seeming regard to the finer points of either humanity or counsel.

The lumbering waiter went round the table and, with a gesture of hostility, thrust the opened box of cigars before each person in turn. Resse hesitated, but fairly certain that Holter was paying for them, took one: Spender did not hesitate: Aiden helped himself to two and winked at the waiter: the judge picked one up, smelled it, and replaced it: Holter took one, stripped off the band, and pierced the end with a match.

'What's to do? Shove 'em on the bill?' asked the waiter.

'Yes,' answered Holter.

'What name?'

'Holter.' Holter sounded rather astonished by the question. 'That will be all, thank you, waiter.'

The waiter lumbered out of the room. After shutting the door behind him, he helped himself to one cigar, hesitated, and then took another.

Holter spoke to the judge. 'I'm sorry you're not smoking. I've always thought that a nice cigar really finishes a meal.'

'I quite agree.'

Holter smiled, showing even teeth. 'We're not all that far from London, Judge, but it seems to be far enough to dry out the cigars.' He picked up the bottle of port, now half empty, and refilled his glass, then carefully sent it round the table in an anti-clockwise direction by passing it to the judge on his right. The Hertonhurst Bar honoured their customs with jealous devotion. Holter called for the loyal toast. 'Mr Junior.'

Aiden stood up and raised his glass. 'Mr Senior, sir, I crave permission to propose the loyal and royal toast?'

'*Gere.*'

'Mr Senior, sir, I give you the loyal and royal toast. To the glorious, pious, and immortal memory of our right noble benefactor: Henry *Secundus, rex magnus, dominus noster.*'

Everyone, but Aiden, remained seated as glasses were raised and the toast repeated. 'Henry *Secundus, rex magnus, dominus noster.*"

'Mr Senior, sir, may we have permission to smoke?' asked Aiden.

'*Gere,*' replied Holter, as he lit his cigar.

Aiden sat down and a few minutes later Holter stood up. 'Mr Junior, it is now my pleasure and privilege to propose the toast, the Hertonhurst Bar. I give you that small but influential circle of individual liberty, that valuable repository of legal independence, that brotherhood without jealousies, the Hertonhurst Bar.' He raised his glass and the others, sitting, did the same. They drank. Holter sat down. 'Would you care to say something on behalf of the Bench, Judge?' he asked.

'I think not,' replied the other.

'It would be an honour. Halsey, just before he died, dined with us and addressed us.'

'Are you asking me to confirm a legal precedent?'

Holter laughed. 'I'm sure, Judge, you'll be on the Bench for quite a time yet.'

'I trust so, even if such extension should be received without pleasure in a number of quarters.'

'No one here, Judge, wishes you anything but a long judicial life.'

'The loyalty of the Hertonhurst Bar is proverbial.'

Holter puffed at his cigar. 'Funny people, Americans,' he said.

'In what way?' asked Spender.

'I met a number of American lawyers the other day and was explaining to them the obvious advantages of an independent judiciary, totally free from any kind of damaging political interference such as they suffer in their country. They questioned this independence on the grounds that the Lord Chancellor is a Cabinet Minister yet appoints JPs, county court judges, and nominates judges of the high court. I tried to explain to them the division between politician and judician – to coin a useful phrase – but I'm certain they couldn't appreciate the point. I feel that a deep sense of tradition is necessary in such matters.'

'Or an even deeper sense of the illogical,' said Resse.

Holter drank some more port. 'I have always maintained that our legal system is every bit as good as it needs to be. If it seems in places illogical, then such apparent illogicality leads to strength, not weakness. Perfection, my dear Oliver, is the last stage before disintegration.'

'Possibly, but in this case you've disintegrated without achieving perfection. You'll have to fine yourself a bottle of wine.'

Holter, who had been about to speak at some length on

the perfections of imperfection, checked himself. He looked as annoyed as he felt. 'What are you talking about?'

'You addressed me by my Christian name.'

'I most certainly did nothing of the kind.'

'On the contrary. And that ill-founded arguing will cost you another.'

Angrily, Holter, who prided himself on knowing all the innumerable rules which governed a mess dinner and observing them, searched his mind for a valid excuse. He scraped the ash from his cigar into the saucer of his coffee cup. 'Judge,' he finally said, 'may one petition you for a verdict?'

'I wasn't listening,' replied the other, and underlined his reply with a long yawn.

'I pray a *tales*,' warned Resse.

'Very well,' snapped Holter, who was unable to forbid this.

'Members of the mess,' said Resse, 'the general issue has been pleaded by the accused *ore tenus* by his verbal denial. So how say you?'

'Guilty,' answered Aiden enthusiastically. 'As guilty as hell.'

'Guilty,' agreed Spender.

'The verdict is unanimous,' said Resse.

Holter's manner changed as if, now that his case was beyond appeal, he wished to show complete magnanimity towards those who had persecuted him. 'You're a right load of bastards. Given half a chance, you'd steal the pennies from a blind man. Never mind, I'll pay the fine which I assess at two bottles of wine. Aiden, go and get the waiter, will you, and ask him to bring them?'

'I'm not so certain it shouldn't be three bottles,' said Resse.

A little of Holter's newly found amiability disappeared. 'Now what's the trouble?'

'Baseless accusations of a vilifying nature. I can prove the legitimacy of my parentage and I feel certain my fellow members can do the same.'

The judge looked at his glass, still three-quarters filled, and decided to enjoy the pleasure of forgoing the rest of the port. The evening, inevitably, had reached the point at which alcohol replaced logic. Twenty years ago, he might have stayed, but now the thought of his bed was far too attractive. 'I must be going, Holter. There's a very full day ahead of us.'

'There certainly is. Good-night, then, Judge. Mr Junior, escort our honoured guest to his car, please, and order the wine.'

Aiden and the judge left the room. Much of Aiden's youthful bounciness was temporarily gone because of the solemn responsibility of escorting one of Her Majesty's high court judges to his official car.

Holter refilled his glass and passed the bottle round the table.

'Old Thwaites gets sourer every year,' said Resse, as he accepted the bottle. 'The milk of human kindness in his breast has turned into vinegar.'

'D'you know,' said Spender, 'he gave my chap seven years the day before yesterday and I'd promised the sentence couldn't possibly be more than two. That kind of thing upsets the delicate counsel-client relationship.'

Resse refilled his glass and passed the bottle on. 'You're all right. There's no need to worry about any kind of relationship with that long a stretch. Who was your solicitor?'

'Seabord. He's a bit of a crook.'

'One's instructing solicitor is never a crook. The more briefs he sends, the more positively virtuous he becomes.' There was a harsh note to Resse's voice.

Holter, never content to be silent for very long, turned round and looked at the closed door. 'Where on earth has the waiter got to with that wine?'

'Are you very eager to pay your fine and so expiate your guilt?' asked Resse.

Before Holter could answer, the waiter came into the room. 'D'you want more drink?' he asked, with typical British provincial surliness.

'We want two bottles of port,' said Holter.

'There ain't any more.'

'Then we'll have two more bottles of the Beaune. If there's any of that remaining?'

'I'll 'ave a look.' The waiter left.

'The service here is getting worse,' said Holter. 'We ought

seriously to consider moving the mess to one of the other hotels.'

'Which one?' replied Resse. 'The Chariot Wheel hasn't any sort of a private room and The White Leopard's food and service is worse than here, if you can conceive such a thing. Bad eating is one of the penalties of belonging to a provincial Bar.'

'The benefits far, far outweigh the disadvantages. The metropolis may, if you'll excuse a harmless *jeu de mots*, make provisions for the gourmet, but it also provides extreme competition: here, in Hertonhurst, we can be a small band of brothers, devoted to our chosen profession, freed from the vice of professional jealousies brought on by overcrowding.'

'Metropolis or provinces, it pays to say the obvious.'

Holter appeared not to have heard.

* * *

Holter lived in Treybrake Hall, a large house six miles from Hertonhurst. The main part had been built in 1709, but in 1827 the owner mistakenly thought it necessary to add an Ionic pillared porch of Homeric dimensions. This porch would have suited one of the ancestral seats in the Shires, but on Treybrake Hall it looked like a folly.

He drove his silver grey Bentley round the left-hand side of the oval drive and across the yard into the garage, which was part of the converted stables. As he switched off the engines, he looked at the dashboard clock. Just after midnight. It had been an enjoyable mess dinner, even if he had slipped up to the extent of being fined a couple of bottles of wine. Still, that was a very small price to pay for tradition. He liked tradition because it anchored the best of the past to the present. The law was a living tradition, to the point of repeated anomalies to those who hadn't the wit to understand, and it reassured him to know he was part of something that was perfect and unchanging.

He climbed out of the Bentley and walked between it and his wife's Mercedes 220 SE to the doors. As he closed and locked the garage, he thought about Resse to whom he had given a lift home: Resse had spent most of the five minutes' drive pointing out what a waste of money it was to drive a luxury car like the Bentley and that no status symbol could be worth so high a price. Resse was a very bitter man.

Holter walked from the garage to the drive and round to the front door. It would have been quicker to enter the house by one of the two back doors, but he preferred not to use them. He passed between two of the massive stone columns, unlocked the door, and went into the hall. He hung his hat in the small cloakroom and went up the broad staircase, past the mounted stags' heads which some guests thought he had shot, to the bedroom.

Charlotte was sitting up in bed, reading.

'Hullo, darling,' she said. 'Did you have a nice evening?'

'Quite pleasant, except that old Thwaites was as sour as ever. And, of course, Oliver was his usual sarcastic self.'

'You must remember how jealous he is of my clever husband.'

He sat down on her side of the bed and stared at her. She was thunderingly beautiful, he thought, his mind somewhat confused by all he had drunk. Her naturally blonde hair framed an oval face that would have inspired Titian: her deep blue eyes made a man feel ten feet tall: her delicately curved mouth was an open invitation. Whenever he looked at her he found it incredible, unbelievable, that he was more than twice her age: he felt only a few years more at the very most.

He began to run the palm of his hand up and down her side and he could feel the warmth of her flesh through the sheer nylon nightdress.

'Did you have a pleasant evening?' he asked, his voice becoming thick.

'Quiet, but interesting. The new dress is a lovely one, Radwick. I'm longing for you to see it.'

'How's Rachael?'

'Quite well, but a little tired.'

'She's an odd woman.' He rested his right hand on her breast.

'You are silly about her.'

'I'm sure she's a Lesbian.'

'That's just ridiculous.' She smiled. 'Just because she dresses like she does and doesn't worry about make-up, it doesn't mean she's queer. Anyway, if she were one, d'you think I'd go on seeing her?'

'You always say she designs the most wonderful clothes, so you might.'

'Darling, you are terrible! I can't think what kind of mind you've got.'

He raised his right hand and tried to slide it down the front of her nightdress. She took hold of it and drew it away from herself. 'It's awfully late, Radwick.'

He tried to replace his hand and felt her strain to prevent him. He became embarrassed, a very different person from the boisterously confident one he had been earlier on. 'What's ... what's the matter, Betty?'

'I'm sorry, Radwick, but I'm rather tired and I'm sure you're the same. Please don't be annoyed, my darling.'

Her nightdress was semi-transparent and the blurred sight of her flesh increased his desires. 'But I'm not too tired. Can't we ...'

'I'd so much rather not now. Don't you think it would be better, anyway, to wait just a little?'

'Why?'

'We don't want it to be like last time, do we?'

He flushed heavily as he drew his hand away from hers. 'All right.'

'Please, please, Radwick, don't get all angry. I hate it when you do that. I was only trying to help both of us. It was because you were so tired last time.'

He stood up, feeling angry because she was so damned attractive and desirable that she made the blood run through his veins as if he were twenty-eight, not fifty-eight. He went into his dressing-room. When he returned to the bedroom, she had switched on his bedside light and switched off hers.

'Good-night, Radwick,' she said. 'Come and kiss me good-night and promise you understand.'

He hesitated, but eventually bent over and kissed her and for several seconds she responded with sensual force. Then, she freed her mouth.

'Good-night, my darling husband,' she said.

He went round the bed and climbed in. For a short while

the fires of desire smouldered in his mind and body, but they soon disappeared as he thought about the next day's work. The murder trial would almost certainly be over by the evening. If the judge had his way, there was no doubt what the verdict was going to be: Mr Justice Thwaites was openly very strong-minded, a fact which caused him frequently to be rebuked by the Court of Criminal Appeal... Not that that ever in the slightest upset him.

Chapter Two

THE EXISTENCE of the Hertonhurst Bar was due to a historical error. Henry II found considerable difficulty in introducing law reforms to that part of Kent because of a small confederation of barons who had discovered that the exclusive right to administer justice could be made a highly profitable one. After four years, the barons were stripped of their lands and rank and one of them, according to the *Hertonhurst Chronicles* which were written about fifty years later, was murdered in Dover Castle by the base use of a red hot poker: a method of death the unfortunate Edward II was later to suffer. Henry II decreed that a special court was to be set up in Hertonhurst so that the inhabitants could once and for all time benefit from pure and unsullied justice. That remarkable king, however, for once made a serious mistake because he appointed a permanent judge who soon discovered that the exclusive right to administer justice could be made a highly profitable one. The court existed over the centuries, eventually becoming an anomaly hallowed by age into an institution. Lawyers became plentiful in Hertonhurst and a 17th century report speaks of a town packed with sewer rats mistakenly termed lawyers who feast on the bones and flesh of unfortunate men and women misguided enough to seek justice or unlucky enough to be dragged to the town to suffer it. Two of these 'sewer rats' were executed during the reign of James II and all the shops and stalls did not trade that day, obviously treating it as a public holiday.

By 1850, the jurisdiction of Hertonhurst Bar had been severely restricted and most of the lawyers had left – rats deserting the sinking ship. In 1856, the Act of Parliament abolished the court except in so far as a court of quarter sessions. On the face of it, the Hertonhurst Bar should have vanished, to become absorbed in the SE Circuit, but by some historical fluke it continued into the twentieth century. In 1928, there were two members, both of whom had private incomes: if they had not, the Bar would have finally vanished. But then there was an unexplained upsurge in litigation and two reasonably successful barristers joined the Bar and brought life back to it. Solicitors rediscovered the advantages of briefing local counsel, not the least of which was the diminution in costs: a diminution solicitors were sometimes decent enough to pass on to the lay clients. In 1945, Radwick Holter joined the Hertonhurst Bar and in 1955 he took Silk. His successes brought more life to the Bar than there had been in the previous hundred years.

Holter was born in that unlikely named Midlands town, Ashby-de-la-Zouch. He was the second of six children and his father had been a blacksmith. Inheriting his mother's quick intelligence, he gained a scholarship to the local grammar school and another from there to Trinity College. He attained a good degree and a 2 (1) in the Bar finals.

Before the Second World War, a man without some private income had to be exceptional to succeed at the Bar: it cost a considerable sum of money to join one of the Inns of Court, a considerable sum to become a pupil in chambers and a far larger sum to live during the initial years when briefs from solicitors were as rare as miracles. Unusual ability or unusual luck, together with tremendous guts, were needed to overcome the disability of poverty. Holter had considerable ability and all the guts in the world because of a blinding desire to succeed. When called to the Bar, he was wearing a hired suit, shoes with badly worn heels, and odd socks. For five years, he worked at night as a dishwasher. After ten years, he had become something of a 'name' as a junior. At forty-eight, against a lot of apparently good advice, he took Silk and within a year it was clear he was never going to regret the move. Before long he was making twenty thousand pounds a year, appearing in courts all over the circuit and in London. He was given more apparently good advice. 'Leave the Hertonhurst Bar and join chambers in London,' but he ignored this just as he had the previous time.

He was a man who dismissed as unimportant the poverty in which he had been born and had lived, but if ever he had been honest with himself on this point he would have admitted he had been indelibly marked by it. The bitterness of it had spurred him on to success and then for ever persuaded him that such success must be shown to all for what it was.

* * *

Josephus Traynton, wearing black coat, striped trousers, stiff white collar, and silver tie, arrived at chambers – on the first floor of Awcott House – at 9.00 AM, just as he had done for the past fifty-six years. For him, 8.59 was early and 9.01 was late. He was a ponderous man, who looked his seventy-one years. He had a large, round face, creased by age, with very definite jowls. He was about to retire and was quite certain that chambers would find it very difficult to continue once he had done so.

He took two keys from his pocket and opened first the heavy wooden door, with the names of the members of chambers on its inner face, and then the second and much lighter built one. He stepped into the rectangular hall-cum-passage. Puffing from the effort involved, he bent down and picked up the mail from the carpet, after which he walked into the clerks' room on the right. He placed the letters on his desk, took off his mackintosh and bowler hat and hung them on the mahogany stand. He returned to his desk, sat down, and sorted out the mail. There was a brief for Resse marked at a mere seven & two, a cheque for Spender in settlement of a long overdue account, a letter from Ashford solicitors reporting the settlement of a case Spender had been advising in, two circulars, and private letters for Holter and Aiden. Traynton's expression became severe as a close examination of the handwriting on the letter to Aiden convinced him that the writer was a young barrister from London who had referred to him, Traynton, as the only living mastodon in captivity, little knowing he was in earshot.

He distributed the letters to the various rooms and by the time he returned to the clerks' room, Marriott had arrived.

'Good morning, good morning, and the top of the world to you,' said Marriott loudly.

'I observe you did not finish the statement of claim in the Fabian case last night,' said Traynton coldly.

'Time pressed so I left it for today.'

'In the old days, a conscientious clerk did not allow time to press.'

'Back in those dark ages, they were still sending little boys up chimneys to sweep 'em, but now, thanks to a thriving capitalistic society, nobody works any more than he bloody well has to.' Marriott at twenty-nine possessed the cockiness of someone who was certain he knew all the answers. He refused to wear black coat and striped trousers, saying such a mournful dress was for undertakers and he appeared instead in patterned suits. He was always careful to make certain the handkerchief in his breast pocket was showing and he knew that only the really uneducated would drink red wine with fish.

Traynton pursued the subject further. 'This is not a job in which a man's work is regulated by a clock. Had I spent all my career looking at my watch . . .'

'The Hertonhurst Bar would have crumbled, nothing at all would ever have got done, and so sing glory Alleluia to Jo-Jo Traynton.'

'That is not amusing.'

'It's all a question of taste, isn't it? Some people laugh at *Punch*, some don't.'

'I dread to think what clients will say when I . . .' Traynton stopped. He was only too aware that in Marriott's eyes he was an ancient relic who needed putting out to grass.

The telephone rang and Traynton answered it. A Maidstone solicitor wanted to know how much Holter would ask to lead in a defended divorce suit at the next assizes. Traynton queried who the client was and, because the answer was evasive, became certain the fee should be a generous one. 'Two hundred and another hundred for the consultation.'

'What? Good God, man, I could get F. E. Smith up from hell for that.'

'We are very busy now.'

'I don't care how busy you are. I've shoved a lot of work Holter's way before now and he can damn' well do this for me now at a reasonable price.'

'I might, sir, as a special concession, drop to a hundred and seventy-five.'

'A hundred.'

'A hundred and seventy-five, sir, and we might call the consultation fifty.'

'You're a blasted thief, Traynton, and it's nothing less than blackmail. I'll tell Holter that when I see him.'

After the call was concluded, Traynton stared down at his desk with a satisfied smile on his heavy face. Marriott would have accepted that brief at a hundred guineas because he had neither the experience nor the intelligence to realize how much it would bear.

Holter, due in court at 10.30, arrived in chambers at 9.30. He went into the clerks' room. ''Morning, Josephus, 'morning, George.' He sat down on the edge of Marriott's desk. 'We had quite a good dinner last night, if one ignores the food. The judge wasn't too objectionable and he left early, so maybe he won't have a liver this morning. Though, God knows, he doesn't need a liver attack to be a bastard in court. Every time I tried to make a point for our chap yesterday, he knocked it aside. Tell me, Josephus, how am I going to get the man off?'

'I confess, sir, that I see little hope for us.'

Holter stood up, crossed the room, and leaned against the marble mantelpiece. His blustering manner covered a character which hated to lose, even when he knew from the beginning that there was small chance of winning: much of his success at the Bar was due to the fact that he never stopped fighting. 'I wonder what kind of witness he'll make in the box?'

'Not very good, sir,' answered Traynton. 'It would be an exaggeration to suppose any part of his story will be believed.'

'Why in the devil did he have to drag the poor woman down and dump her body beneath that photo of himself? No jury goes for that sort of thing, Josephus.'

'No, sir. Especially as he had a good education.'

'It was a frenzy of love,' said Marriott. 'She enjoyed herself with another bloke, so he knocks her on the head and drags her body in front of his photograph to show what he thinks of her. If I was on the jury, I'd acquit him for showing some real passion.'

'That is hardly a responsible and proper attitude,' said Traynton, with a loud sniff.

Holter jerked himself upright, and walked across to the door.

'Mr Drift is sending a defended divorce, sir,' said Traynton.

'As long as the fee's high enough,' answered Holter without interest as he left. He went into his own room, to the right of the corridor, and crossed to the window. The main road was as clogged with traffic as ever, despite the by-pass, and as he watched a policeman appeared and tried to ease a right-turning car across the far line of cars. He thought about the case and became angry because he knew that so far his advocacy had been useless: then his mind switched to the previous night and he remembered how Charlotte had refused him, and why, and that made him angrier because he hated to think of himself as anything but successful.

He turned away from the window and sat down in the leather-covered chair behind his massive and expensive desk. On his right was the wall cabinet with glass doors in which were the visible, macabre proofs of his previous successes against all the odds: the murder weapons from cases he had won.

He stared at the photographic portrait of Charlotte which was on the corner of his desk. The photographer had brilliantly captured her striking, exotic beauty and the smile which had, until she agreed to marry him, tormented him with an aching longing. He remembered her as she had been when he first met her, not exactly poor but not able to buy the kind of clothes and jewellery her beauty so obviously called for. Thank God, he thought, he had had the sense not to think of marriage until he could afford the luxury. Oliver Resse had married the same year he was called to the Bar and ever since then he and his wife had had to make do and mend, which must have been extremely galling for her since she came from a very well known county family.

He looked away from Charlotte's photograph and switched his mind back to work. When the trial resumed, he would have to open the case for the defence and put Albert Smith in the witness-box. What could they do to help save the man?

* * *

Albert Smith resembled no Romeo, no Paris, swept by the burning fires of passion: he was small, round-shouldered, mean-faced, and his wispy moustache was the same indeterminate colour as his rapidly thinning hair. His life was a recorded failure, first as a schoolboy, then as an articled clerk, finally as a husband. One day, when he knew all about middle age, he met a woman in a pub near Coninden and was immediately captured by her broad, jolly vulgarity: captured to such an extent that two weeks later he made a half-hearted attempt to seduce her. He was astonished when he met nothing but encouragement. He loved her passionately and talked about gaining a divorce. Then, one afternoon, he visited her house when he had not been expected and he found obvious signs that he was not the only recipient of her favours. He clubbed her to death with a poker, dragged her body from the bedroom to the sitting-room and left it under the photograph of himself which she had always said was her most treasured possession. He went home and told his wife everything, tearfully complaining about the unfaithfulness of his late mistress.

In the witness-box, Albert Smith looked incapable of killing anything larger than a mosquito.

Holter fought hard and long for the defence, but the jury were plainly against him and the judge, looking in his robes and wig to be quite incapable of erroneous human emotions, did not hesitate to underline the defects in the defence's version of what had happened.

'When ... When there was no answer, I went into the house,' said the prisoner.

Holter concealed his contempt for Smith. Smith was a failure and he, Holter, hated failures. That was why he had in the past fifteen years only once returned to Ashby-de-la-Zouch to see his brothers and sisters. 'Will you please describe what you did on entering the house?'

'I called out "Jane" and there wasn't any answer.'

'Did that worry you at all?' asked the judge, with a tired sarcasm which could never appear in the transcripts, but which plainly told the jury what he thought of such ridiculous evidence.

'Worry ... worry me?' said Smith.

'Never mind.'

Holter spoke. 'Perhaps, my lord, it would be better if the accused were left to tell us in his own words what happened?'

'Better for whom, Mr Holter?'

Holter addressed Smith again. 'What did you do when there wasn't any answer?'

'I went into the sitting-room.'

'And?'

'She wasn't there.' He said this with such an air of pained surprise that someone laughed. He hastily went on speaking. 'I ... I went up the stairs to her bedroom.' He began to stutter. 'When I look ... looked in I saw her. She ... she was on the floor, dead. I swear she was ... was dead. You ... you've got to believe me.'

'It is not your own counsel you have to convince,' commented the judge. 'It is the jury.'

'My lord, I really must object,' said Holter.

'Very well.'

'It is most damaging for the Bench to suggest such an implication.'

'What am I supposed to have implied, Mr Holter?'

Holter wisely forbade to answer. He turned to face the witness-box. 'What did you do when you discovered she was dead?'

'I couldn't believe it was true. I knew I had to get her to a doctor so I carried her downstairs.'

Holter stared at the prisoner and wondered how any man could be such a fool as to say that? Hadn't they tried to tell him in the consultations that jurymen might be stupid, but juries usually had a certain amount of collective commonsense? 'Where did you put her downstairs?'

'In the sitting-room.'

'Whereabouts?'

'I ... I was going to put her on the sofa, but I couldn't, so I laid her carefully on the floor.'

Holter looked down at his brief. His solicitor, sitting in front, turned round and grimaced. Holter put another question. 'Did you place her near anything?'

'Just on the floor.'

'Not in any one particular part of the floor?'

'No.'

'We have heard evidence that the dead woman's body was discovered immediately underneath a photograph of you. Did you know you were leaving her near this photograph?'

'No. No. I swear I didn't. I didn't know what I was doing.'

'You are saying, then, that the fact the dead woman was found beneath your photograph was pure coincidence and not, as the prosecution alleges, a symbolic gesture of hate?'

'No,' mumbled the prisoner. No man had ever made a more patently false denial.

* * *

Fifteen days later, on a June day so warm that he had actually left his umbrella at home, Josephus Traynton arrived in chambers as the church clock was striking nine o'clock. He took the two keys from his pocket and inserted the larger one in the lock of the outer, wooden door. When he tried to turn it, nothing moved. Frowning, he stared down at the lock and thought sadly how everything had changed since he was a boy and then he removed the key, visually inspected it, and re-inserted it. Again he tried to turn the tumblers and again they did not move. Muttering angrily, he went to pull the key free, but because it was not exactly lined up with the keyhole it caught on the lock plates. The door swung open.

He was shocked. There were certain verities in life and when any one of them ceased to be it was as if the world had denied part of itself. An even more cataclysmic thought occurred to him – suppose the inner door was also unlocked so that throughout the night anyone in Hertonhurst could have walked into chambers and poked and pried amongst all the papers? Almost afraid to do so, he turned the handle of the inner door and pushed. It opened.

He shuffled forward, bent down and picked up the mail and went into the clerks' room which, somewhat to his astonishment, was exactly as he had left it the previous night. He hung his bowler hat on the nearest hook, checked in the mirror that his tie was neat and tidy, and sat down at his desk to open the mail. There were three new briefs which gave him great pleasure, not because his own income was thereby augmented by a shilling in every pound, but because the success of members was his success.

He read through four letters that were addressed to him. A firm of solicitors were disputing the statement of fees he had sent them. Since he had not once been wrong in his thirty-five years as chief clerk, he ignored the accusation.

He picked up the private letters for Holter and Resse and left. He first went into Resse's room and put the two letters on the larger of the two desks, then walked along to Holter's room. He entered, crossed to the desk, and was about to put the letters down when he looked to the right at something which until then had been hidden by the desk. On the floor was the body of a man whose head was partially missing.

Chapter Three

TRAYNTON PUT the letters down on the desk. He moved them fractionally to the left so that they were perfectly in line with the blotter. He stood upright and for a while did not look to his right. If the body was still there when he looked again, it meant that his world was for ever wrecked and lost – things like murders happened, but not in chambers. He looked through the large window at the traffic-clogged High Street, more clogged then ever because electricity workmen were digging up part of it only two months after the waterboard workmen had done the same.

Very slowly, he looked to his right, but keeping his gaze above the floor. He saw the cabinet in which Mr Holter kept his gruesome mementoes. He did not hold with anything so extrovert as this collection: a gentleman would not have so boldly displayed the symbols of his success. But, of course, Mr Holter although highly successful was not a gentleman. Traynton had stared at the cabinet for quite some time before he realized that the doors were wide open. He shivered and then, like a man suddenly plucking up all his courage before he was left with none, looked down at the floor. The body was still there. He was used to seeing police photographs of the savaged corpses of men and women, but lacking the comforting impersonality of a photograph, he began to feel sick at the sight before him.

He turned away and walked very slowly to the door. He looked back, but it was still all there and he went out into the corridor and shut the door behind him as silently as possible.

Fifty-six years spent in the service of the law had not prepared him for this and he was far too bewildered to think clearly. In such a crisis, he could conceive of only one thing to do and that was to ring Mr Holter.

Once in the clerks' room, he picked up the telephone and – after a wild moment in which his memory seemed completely to have deserted him – dialled Mr Holter's number. As the dialling tone began, he nervously tapped on the desk with his fingers. Why, he wondered bitterly, couldn't this have waited until after he had retired? Surely the life he had led had been exemplary enough to ensure better treatment to him that this?'

The connection was made. 'Yes?' said a woman's voice.

On Traynton's heavy, bulbous face there appeared an expression of dislike. Mr Holter was not the kind of wife a leading Silk should have: a leading Silk's wife should be mature, poised, and beyond doubt a lady. In any case, there was something lubriciously embarrassing about a man of fifty-eight being married to a woman of twenty-six. 'Mrs Holter, this is Traynton speaking. Might I please speak to Mr Holter?'

'Why?'

'I should very much like a word with him, Madam.'

'Yes, but what about?'

'Work, Madam.'

After a short pause, she said she would go and find him. As he waited, Traynton wondered whether he could allow himself a cigarette before luncheon, contrary to all custom, in view of the quite shattering nature of the events of the morning. He had taken hold of the packet in his coat pocket when Holter spoke over the phone.

'What is it, Josephus? Damn it, man, it's far too early to listen to your moaning.'

Traynton's voice became more pompous than ever. 'A very grave matter has arisen, sir, which I considered you must be acquainted with immediately.'

'I'll be in chambers in half an hour. Why can't it wait that long?'

'It cannot wait at all, sir.'

'All right, all right, what is it? I'll swear you get a positively perverse pleasure from covering me with your gloom first thing in the morning.'

'Someone is dead, sir.'

'Well? It comes to all of us.'
'Not in chambers, sir.'
'How d'you mean?'
'There is a dead man in your room, sir, just by your desk and on the right hand side of it if one faces the road. His head has been severely damaged and there is a great deal of blood. It is all extremely unpleasant.'

There was a pause. 'Josephus, have you been drinking?'

'Sir, I do not drink before lunch-time, nor ever when I am working. I deeply resent the suggestion.'

'Then you're seeing things. How in the name of hell could a dead man get into chambers?'

'I have no idea, sir. However, he has.'

'Have you told the police?'

'No, sir, not yet.'

'Then get on to them immediately.'

'Very well, sir.'

'Who's dead?'

'I did not make a close investigation, sir, and the head was turned away from me. His head, sir, is in a mess.'

After that call was over, Traynton dialled O, there being no 999 call on the Hertonhurst exchange. As the dialling tone began, Marriott walked into the room. Traynton used his free arm to produce his gold hunter from his waistcoat pocket and open the cover. 'You are nearly fifteen minutes late,' he said.

*   *   *

Holter always drove without any regard whatsoever to other road users. Secure within the Bentley, the supreme status symbol, he was convinced that everyone should, and would, give way to him. Somehow, he had never had any but a minor accident. His drive to chambers that morning was more recklessly careless than usual.

He parked in a small side road and walked from that to the High Street and Awcott House, a three story early Victorian building, once a private house, set back from the pavement and separated from it by a small lawn and two very small flower beds.

He went in and up to the first floor, entered chambers. 'Josephus,' he called out.

Traynton came out of the clerks' room. 'Good morning, sir,' he said, in sepulchral tones of voice. 'A policeman is present, sir.'

'Where?'

'In your room, sir.'

'Does anyone know who it is yet?'

'No, sir.'

'What a hell of a mess. How the devil did he get into chambers?'

'The outer doors of chambers were unlocked this morning, sir. I regret to have to inform you that you must have forgotten to lock them last night when you and Mr Corry left.'

'Don't be so damn' silly. Of course I locked them.' Holter lit a cigarette. 'What smashed in the man's head?'

'I've no idea, sir.'

'Who's in chambers now?'

'Apart from us, sir, Marriott and the policeman in your room. I understand he has rung the police station for assistance.'

'I'd better go and see what's what.' As Holter crossed to the door of his room, he wondered what he was going to find. Traynton was normally a good chief clerk, but he could be reduced to a fool by the unexpected. Still, however much of a fool he was being today, it was impossible to believe he could mistake anything for a bloody corpse.

He opened the door and stepped inside.

A uniformed constable turned to see the smartly dressed, slightly portly figure. 'You can't come in here,' he said hurriedly.

Holter ignored the constable and walked to his desk. When he reached his chair, he was able to see the crumpled figure, the head in a pool of blood, lying on the floor. Something about the figure was familiar. He felt repulsed by the bloody shapelessness of the man.

'Are you Mr Holter?' asked the constable.

'Yes.'

'I'm sorry, sir, but you'll have to get out of here.'

'D'you know who that is?'

'No, sir. Never seen him before.'

The door opened and two men, in civilian clothes,

entered. One was large, but not fat, and the other was shorter and thinner, with a narrow face set in bitter lines. This second man carried a suitcase.

'Good morning, Mr Holter,' said the larger man.

' 'Morning.' Holter stared at him, frowning slightly.

'Detective Inspector Brock, sir. We've met once or twice in court. This is Detective Sergeant Peach.'

'What the hell's he doing here in my room?' Holter pointed at the dead man.

'That's one of the things we shall be finding out, sir. Any idea who the dead man is?'

'I haven't seen his face yet, but the clothes seem familiar. Goddamn it, what the hell's he doing here?'

'Lying dead,' said the detective sergeant surlily.

'Just before you go, sir,' said Brock, with undiminished politeness, 'would you have a look at his face in case you can name him? Walk round over there if you will and don't come any nearer to him than you are now.'

Holter went round the far side of the desk until he could see the face: he recognized it and immediately felt as if he had lost touch with reality. There was an entry wound between the right eye and ear and the opposite side of the head was a mess.

'You know him, sir,' said the detective inspector, more as a statement of fact than a question.

'It's Corry.'

'Who's he?'

'Lawrence Corry, the solicitor. He ... he was here last night.'

'About what time?'

'Until we left in the evening. We were discussing a case in which he wanted an opinion. My junior couldn't get here – case in Sevenoaks – so we carried on without him.'

'When did you leave here?'

'Some time after six.'

'D'you know whether you two were the last to go out, sir?'

'Yes, we were.'

'Thanks for your help, sir. I'm afraid you'll have to leave us now.'

Holter looked away from the dead man. 'I need all my papers...' he began.

'We'll free them just as soon as we can, sir, but I'm afraid that just for the moment you'll have to leave them with us unless there's anything of very great urgency?'

'There's nothing immediate.' Without thinking, he stubbed out the cigarette he had previously been smoking and now he lit another. 'It's ... odd, seeing him lie there, dead. Last time I saw him he was walking down the High Street and now he's there, dead.'

'It's always a strange metamorphosis, sir.'

Holter walked back round the desk to the door. When he next spoke, his voice had regained all its old authority. 'I shall want the set of papers on my blotter by lunch-time at the latest, Inspector. I'm in court tomorrow morning and I'll have to work on them. You'll please see my clerk has them in good time.' He turned and left the room.

The detective sergeant crossed to the desk and put the case down on it. 'He's a right proper bastard.'

'Old Holter? Last time we faced each other in court he tore me up for confetti and threw the bits out of the window. I spoke the truth and the jury didn't believe a word of it.'

'He's good at destroying the truth.'

Brock looked at his detective sergeant and, not for the first time, thought that if the other had had even the suspicion of a sense of humour he would have risen higher in the police force than he had.

Brock very slowly went round the room, visually searching every inch of the floor. When he came to the cabinet on the wall, he stared at the various objects which hung inside: a cosh made from an Underground train strap, a commando dagger with rust coloured stains on its blued blade, a home-made pistol built out of a length of gas pipe, a half-shattered mouse-trap that had been rigged up as a mechanical fuse, a broad-bladed sheath-knife the top of which had been broken off, and a small glass phial containing a rough powder. It needed little imagination on his part to guess what those objects were: indeed, he seemed to remember being told that Holter invariably pinched the murder weapon and then blandly denied all or any knowledge of its whereabouts.

Corry had been shot. There were several empty hooks in the cabinet and a revolver or automatic could have hung on any one of them.

Brock knelt down on the carpet, near one of the leather chairs in front of the desk. The only place where a gun could be, if still in the room, was under the desk or one of the chairs. As he pressed his cheek on to the carpet and looked under the chair farthest to his left, he saw a revolver.

He stood up and dusted the knees of his trousers. He stared at the body and at the chair under which was the revolver, memorizing the relative positions even though they would be both sketched and photographed. After a while, he spoke. 'There's a revolver under there, Peach. At a rough guess, it's a four five five Webley. We'll leave it until the photographer's done his chore.'

'D'you know what?'

'No doubt you'll tell me.'

'I'd give a fiver to land this job round that snooty bastard's neck.'

'Don't get too generous, too soon,' replied Brock. 'Or maybe you didn't notice that bruise on Holter's neck?'

Chapter Four

HOLTER WALKED to the window of the clerks' room and looked down at the High Street. After a moment, he turned. 'Who in the hell would want to kill Corry?'

'Everyone who knew him,' replied Resse.

'Nobody, barrister or solicitor, even began to like him,' said Marriott. With a gesture frequently repeated, he ran the palm of his hand over his swept-back black hair.

'You should not speak like that,' said Traynton severely.

'*De mortuis nil nisi bonum*, Josephus?' queried Resse ironically.

'I just do not hold with criticizing members of the profession, sir, even if they are solicitors.' Traynton, sitting at his desk, glared at Marriott as he tried to indicate to the other that a clerk's duty at such a moment as the present one was to remain silent.

'But you must admit that in his case it's a pleasure to do so,' said Resse.

'I admit, with very great respect, sir, no such thing.'

'Oh, well, every man to his tastes, as the bishop said to the hermaphrodite. Josephus, how much has he died owing me?'

'A considerable sum, sir.'

'What are the odds of getting any of it paid?'

'I should not wish to prognosticate, sir.'

'Maybe his personal representatives will have a kinder heart than he did.' Resse tried to speak lightly, but his voice was harsh.

Holter spoke to Resse. 'Has he been giving you a lot of work?'

'A considerable amount, Radwick. Although I hasten to add that the word "considerable" has pertinence only for me. For you, the correct description would be chicken-feed.'

Holter shrugged his shoulders. Resse's income was only a tithe of his own and Resse had the kind of character which publicly made light of the fact but secretly was embittered by it. Resse was the more clever lawyer of the two, but to be a clever lawyer was the least of the prerequisites to becoming a successful barrister.

There was a pause, broken by Marriott. 'D'you think he committed suicide?'

'I very much doubt he had sufficient consideration for the rest of the world,' said Resse.

'But unless it was an accident, then it must be...'

'Murder? Why not? Corry was born to be murdered. He was thoroughly dislikeable and he was a solicitor. Who could resist such a combination?'

Holter walked from the window to Traynton's desk. 'I can't blasted well get into my own room because of him.'

Traynton looked up. 'It's the Fastney case tomorrow morning, sir.'

'I know, I know. Don't go on and on underlining the obvious.'

The bell of the outside door rang. Breathing deeply, Traynton stood up and, with measured strides, left the room. He returned seconds later and spoke to Holter. 'A reporter, sir, who had the impudence to ask to come into chambers and speak to people. I assured him of the impossibility of his proposal.'

Holter made some muttered reply and then stepped over to the mantelpiece and examined his reflection in the mirror which hung just above it. Satisfied by what he saw, he transferred his attention to the briefs on the mantelpiece and picked one up. 'Fifty guineas for Alan – he's moving up in the world, isn't he?'

'That brief, sir,' replied Traynton, 'is from the firm in which his brother is a partner.'

'The advantages of nepotism,' said Resse, 'or how to become a successful barrister without really trying.'

Holter had already lost interest in the markings of Spender's brief. He tried to recall to mind his departure from chambers the previous night. He and Corry had left the room and gone into the corridor. He had looked quickly into the clerk's room, it had been empty, and then they had both gone out. For the moment, he couldn't remember locking the doors, but it was inconceivable that he hadn't done so.

* * *

The detective constable who was finger-print expert and photographer took the last photograph and then packed the large camera in its case. He folded up the tripod. 'All right to pull out the gun from under the chair, sir, and test?'

'Yep.' Brock fingered the money in his trouser pocket as he turned and spoke to the middle-aged, grey-haired man waiting with obvious impatience by the doorway. 'OK now, sir, and thanks for waiting.'

The police surgeon picked up his bag, crossed the floor to the body, and knelt down to begin his examination. After a while, he looked up. 'There's no evidence of powder blackening or tattooing and the entrance wound hasn't been washed either by the blood or with water. I'll give you five to one, here and now, it wasn't suicide. The body will have to be taken down to the morgue for a full PM before anyone can be certain, but until then you can say that the muzzle of the gun was more than a foot from his head when it was fired. In thirty years, I've never yet heard of a suicide holding the gun away from himself.'

'But I suppose there could always be a first time?'

'Only if the man's too mental not to worry about missing.'

'Any idea, sir, of the maximum distance at which a person can hold a gun and aim it at himself?'

'Twenty inches.' The doctor returned to his examination of the body.

The detective constable had brought the revolver out from under the chair and was now holding it by the corrugated side plates of the butt. He laid it carefully on a large sheet of grey paper. Finger-prints were so very seldom found on guns, because of the lack of smooth recording surfaces, that the task of searching for them was almost certainly a hopeless one, yet it had to be carried out. The detective dusted the revolver with a light coloured powder.

Brock leaned against the desk as he studied the room, trying to saturate his mind with the picture of what he saw. This was probably a murder case and that made it the biggest kind of case any police officer could be landed with. There would be a mass of publicity, especially since people like Holter were mixed up in it. Success would boost his, Brock's, chances of promotion, failure might for ever damn them. He was a very ambitious man who, so far, had done nothing which might deny his ambitions and this case must not be allowed to change that. His thoughts were interrupted by the detective constable.

'There aren't any prints on the gun. Only a few smudges and smears which don't add up to a thing.'

'OK.' Brock crossed to the small table and picked up the revolver. He broke it. The central ejector spindle rose and ejected six cartridges: three were empty cases, three were unfired. He held all six cartridges in the palm of his hand, turned and stared round the room. One cartridge was known to have been fired: the bullet had gone through the dead man's head, creating a far more extensive exit than entry wound, and had then become lodged in the top of one of the bookcases, out of which it would have to be dug. No other bullet holes had been found. He smelled each of the three empty cases in turn and thought that only one of them had recently been fired. A laboratory test would confirm or deny this assumption, but Holter's evidence might equally well do so sooner.

Detective Sergeant Peach, carrying a portable searchlight, came into the room. 'Had a hell of a job finding this, sir,' he said, as he put it down on the carpet.

Brock ignored the moan. Peach was a man who enjoyed a miserable delight in finding the world always full of difficulties. 'Get it working as quickly as you like.'

Peach switched on the searchlight and trained the beam along the carpet, which stretched to within two feet of each wall. The beam crossed the dead man's body and the doctor looked round angrily and asked them to leave him to do his job without interference.

Brock made a conciliatory apology and then ordered Peach to begin a visual search of the carpet. Hardly had the beam moved away from the bookcase to the right of the door when Peach spoke.

'There's something there, sir, between the books and the desk.'

'Such as?'

'It's in the carpet and showing pinkish.'

Brock moved until he could look along the line of the beam and he saw a patch of colour that to him was more white than pink. He went up to this patch and knelt down by it. There were traces of a finely grained powder in the pile of the carpet. He smelled the powder and there was a definite impression of a pleasing scent, although he could not identify it. The odds were, then, that this was a face powder. 'We'll have to use a vacuum pick-up for this,' he said, as he took a pencil from his pocket and laid it down on the carpet as a marker.

Peach swung the beam of light along the carpet, away from Brock, who stayed where he was for several seconds before standing up.

Peach spoke again, this time excitedly. 'There's a trail from that point, there, to the body.' In his enthusiasm, he swung the light round too far and the lower half of the doctor was once more bathed in the harsh light. Hastily, Peach altered the set of the beam.

Brock crossed the room to stand by Peach's side and seconds later the doctor left the body and, walking right round the desk, joined them.

They could see, quite clearly, the irregular, wavy line which led from near the cabinet on the wall to the body, crumpled up in death. It looked as if it had been made by a glossy varnish and although it would need a laboratory test to be certain, none of them doubted it was a trail of blood.

'Well, Doc.,' asked Brock, 'could he have crawled towards the door after being shot?'

The doctor fingered the side of his chin. 'That's another answer only the PM will be able to give you, Inspector, when it's certain what the damage to the head is, but speaking off the cuff I'd say he didn't move an inch of his own accord after being shot.'

'Then we've got the problem of why he was moved that far after death?'

'You have, Inspector, I've no wish to teach you your job, but are you thinking of calling in the pathologist before the body's moved?'

'Yes, sir.'

'Very wise.' He turned and looked at the small patch of shattered woodwork in the bookcase to the left of the door. 'You know, allowing the man was standing at the beginning of the trail that bullet hole now makes sense, but where the body is, it doesn't. Odd to drag the body so far and no farther.'

'Anything to make the case bloody difficult,' muttered Peach.

* * *

As Joan Fleming crossed from the stairs to the door of chambers, two men moved forward from where they had been waiting. 'Going in there, love?' asked the elder.

She lifted her head slightly. 'That's my business.'

'Sure. But we'd like to make it ours as well. You see, we can't get anywhere with that old fool inside.'

Her curiosity battled with her over-developed sense of propriety, and lost. 'D'you mean Mr Traynton, the chief clerk?'

'Acts as if he was pregnant with the eleventh commandment. When we said we were just honest reporters...'

'Reporters?'

'That's right, love. We present one half of the world to the other half and stand back and listen to the howls. How about telling us what's going on inside?'

'But why should anything? I mean, I don't know of anything.'

'You don't? Thought you must work here?'

'Well, I do. But not full time, like. My husband...' She paused, to underline this word. 'You see, my husband doesn't like me to have to leave home early in the morning.'

'If I was lucky enough to be married to you, love, I wouldn't want you to leave home, ever.'

She tried to appear contemptuous of so rank a compliment, but could not quite hide her pleased satisfaction.

'You didn't know they'd found a dead body inside, love?'

'They've what?'

'Found a dead man. But we can't make out who, why, when, what, or how. You could help us.'

She reached up and patted her hair.

'Suppose you were to go in and find out what's what and come back out here and let us know? We'd be very grateful, if you understand?' Over many years, the reporter had found how useful a phrase that was since it promised all things to all people.

'I'll see what I can do,' she answered, wondering if she had remembered to make-up properly.

'There's my favourite brunette.' He rang the doorbell. 'They've locked the door and are only admitting honest callers.'

The door was opened by a uniformed constable. 'I've already told you...' He began.

'It's not for us,' replied the reporter, 'but for this lovely young lady.'

The constable looked at her. 'Can I help you, Miss?'

'It's not Miss, it's Mrs. And since I work here, you can't do nothing but let me in,' she answered pertly, as she walked past him. She went into the clerks' room and spoke excitedly to Marriott who was making out one of the fees books. 'Here, George, what's up? There are a couple of blokes outside who say they're reporters and that there's someone dead in here.'

Traynton, sitting at his desk, looked up. 'There has been a most unfortunate occurrence, Mrs Fleming. Mr Corry has met an untimely demise.'

'D'you mean he's dead?'

'Won't get no deader,' said Marriott.

'Go on! What ever happened?' She put her handbag down on the small typing table at which she sat. At that moment, there was a buzz from the switchboard which was at the back of the table. 'What was to do? Heart? My uncle dropped down dead just as quick as you like. He was eating a meringue and his false teeth got stuck and he was trying to pull 'em out...'

'The telephone has sounded,' said Traynton.

'They can wait,' she answered, but even as she spoke she plugged in one of the cables. 'In the end, they had to take 'em right out before they could get 'em out of the meringue.'

Holter hurried into the room. 'Josephus, where the hell are those papers? If I'm in court tomorrow, I must have them now. Go and get them.'

'Very well, sir.'

'And telephone Alfred and tell him that the statement of claim is so much poppycock. If I couldn't have drawn up something better than that when I was a junior, I'd have applied for a post with one of the oil companies.'

'To which case are you referring, sir?'

'The Hawkesley case, of course. And while we're on the subject, what made you accept a mere hundred for it? The plaintiff has more money than he knows what to do with.'

'I considered, sir, that one hundred guineas was the right and proper fee.'

'I wish you'd realize money isn't worth as much now as it was fifty years ago.'

Traynton majestically forbore to answer.

'When you've got my papers off the desk, Josephus, ask the police how much longer they think they're going to be around?' Holter left the room in as much of a rush as he had entered it.

Traynton stood up. 'There is some typing for you, Mrs Fleming. One petition for a divorce and a defence.'

She sat down and took the cover off the typewriter. 'What's the divorce – nice and juicy?'

'Were it of such a nature, you would not be asked to deal with it,' he replied with crushing finality as he left the room.

She spoke to Marriott. 'He's a proper spoil-sport. As I always say, a nice bit of spice makes life interesting.'

'Yes.'

'Here – what's the matter with you? You're the first to have a good giggle in a nullity case with a husband what can't nohow.'

He brushed his hand across his brow. 'They say half his head's missing.'

'Who?'

'Mr Corry.'

'Him? Go on! I thought it was a heart attack? Well, it don't do to get all mournful. Here today and gone tomorrow, that's what I always say. Did he fall over, or something?'

'He was shot.'

'Shot!' She stared in complete amazement at Marriott.

In the corridor outside the clerks' room, Brock was kneeling by the inner front door and assembling a lock probe. A uniformed constable stood by him, a small dry battery in his hand.

Traynton, standing three feet from the others, spoke. 'Mr Holter must have those papers.'

Brock answered without looking up. 'He'll have them in good time.'

'If they are not forthcoming within the next fifteen minutes, I shall go and collect them.'

Brock screwed together the two halves of the probe. 'You won't, you know,' he said equably.

'I would remind you, Inspector, you are not dealing with the *hoi polloi*. We in chambers know our legal rights.'

'It would be a fat lot of use coming to you for advice if you didn't.'

'You have no right to hold on to those papers. If you continue unlawfully to do so, we shall be forced to bring an action for conversion, replevin, trespass, detinue, or specific restitution. I might perhaps remind you ...'

Brock looked up. 'You wouldn't want to be charged with obstructing a police officer in the course of his duty, contrary to section thirty-eight of the Offences against the Person Act, would you?'

Traynton began to object indignantly, but became silent when his objections were ignored. Much against his will, he became engrossed in what the detective was doing and remained to watch.

Brock was handed the battery and he connected it to the two wires from the probe, a tiny tube a foot long with a minute bulb and mirror one end of it and a magnifying lens the other.

Using the handle, Brock slowly inserted the end of the probe into the keyhole of the mortice action lock. He switched on the battery and peered into the tiny magnifying lens, systematically moving the probe up and down and from side to side.

After a couple of minutes, he withdrew the probe and passed it to the constable.

'What are you doing?' asked Traynton, whose curiosity became too great for the dignified silence he had wanted to maintain.

'Searching the inside of the lock for scratches.'

'Why?'

'Because if they're conspicuous by their absence, it means the lock wasn't forced last night and if the lock wasn't forced then it's pretty certain, isn't it, that if Corry left chambers he came back with someone who had a key?'

'Are there any scratches?'

'No.'

'But ... but that means ...'

'Quite,' answered Brock.

Chapter Five

SPENDER'S ROOM was the smallest in chambers and such space as there was was reduced by two large freestanding bookcases which contained a miscellany of text books, many of which dated back to the beginning of the century. Spender was in Ashford, defending a man who had drunk too many whiskies and then had had the misfortune to crash into a stationary police car. Holter had temporarily moved into Spender's room. After examining the markings of the briefs on the desk, Holter swept them to one side and put his own papers in the cleared space.

He liked to have a rough list of questions he would put to witnesses and he was preparing this for the next day when there was a knock on the door and Brock walked in, followed by someone Holter had not previously seen.

'This is Detective Constable Squire,' said Brock.

Holter briefly studied the newcomer and saw a man of thirty who was dressed in a badly cut suit.

'I wondered if you had a minute or two to spare, sir?' said Brock.

'I'm very busy.' Holter looked at his watch. 'In any case, it's almost lunch-time.'

'I won't keep you long.' Holter muttered something which Brock chose to take as an invitation to sit down in one of the two uncomfortable wooden chairs before the desk. 'Was there a four fifty-five Webley revolver in that collection of yours in the cupboard on the wall?'

'Yes.'

'I suppose it was from one of your previous cases?'

'It was. That double murder at Bonnington four or five years ago.'

'Were there any cartridges in the gun or somewhere in the cabinet?'

'Why are you asking?'

'That was the gun which shot Corry.'

'Was it?' Holter frowned slightly.

'Was the gun loaded, sir?'

'It was just as it was found at the murder. Two rounds had been fired and the other four hadn't. The man was an exceptional marksman.'

'Wasn't it very dangerous to keep a loaded gun in that cabinet?'

'I never considered it so.'

'Who knew it was loaded?'

Holter picked up a pencil and underlined a sentence in the typed proof of one of the witnesses in the next day's trial. 'I couldn't answer that.'

'But you could try.'

'Could I?'

'Did you make a secret of the fact it was loaded?'

'I neither broadcast it, nor hid it.'

'I suppose, though, we can say that the casual caller would hardly expect it to be loaded?'

'We don't have casual callers in chambers.'

Brock nodded his head, as if in agreement. 'I hope, sir, you won't mind if we test your hands?'

'Test them?' queried Holter sharply.

'You'll know how it's sometimes possible to check if a person's recently fired a gun? The boffins have just brought out a jelly which is supposed to be much simpler and more efficient than the old paraffin test. The jelly changes colour if the hand has on it any appreciable quantity of burned particles.'

Holter put down the pencil. 'I have not recently fired a gun.'

'No, sir,' agreed Brock politely. Then he added, as if he really meant it: 'You won't have the fun of seeing the jelly change colour.'

'Why do you suspect a member of chambers, as you so obviously do?'

'I'm having the locks of the front doors taken off, sir, so that we can open them up and give them a complete examination, but I'm willing to go on record now to say they weren't forced last night.'

'Either you're wrong, or someone outside chambers has somehow obtained the necessary keys.' Holter carefully folded up the proof he had been working on, bundled it up with all the other papers and re-tied the red tape. He stood up. 'Inspector, do you know anything about the Bar?'

'I'm tempted to answer, enough,' replied Brock, with quiet sarcasm.

'Members of the Bar are professional brothers, both by inclination and tradition. In this day and age, a lot of people are misguided enough to jeer at the mention of a dedicated profession, but that is what I unashamedly call it. We are dedicated to seeing that justice is done.'

'Possibly, sir. The one trouble might be to decide what justice means.'

'There's absolutely no ambiguity. Justice is what is dispensed in our courts of law.'

'Yes, sir, but that changes according to which part of the court you sit or stand in.'

'I don't understand.'

Wisely, Brock argued no further, but tried to change the conversation. 'What you're really saying is that you don't think anyone in chambers could have killed Corry?'

'I am saying that people who are dedicated to seeing that justice is done are not going to go out of their way to commit a terrible crime.'

'Passions do sometimes alter people.'

'Not barristers.'

'How did you like Corry, sir?'

'I will be utterly frank. He was not a man to like.'

'D'you think anyone around here disliked him enough to kill him?'

'I thought I'd already given my opinion on that. In any case, my answer could not possibly be in the nature of evidence.'

Brock smiled his quick smile, which seemed to alter the whole set of his large face. 'You know far more than me about courtroom evidence, sir, but I'll stick my neck out and say I know a bit more about what kind of evidence is necessary to get someone to that courtroom. D'you know of anyone who hated Corry?'

The telephone sounded once, which was Holter's signal. He picked up the receiver. 'Yes?'

'Radwick, what's happened?' asked Charlotte, almost breathlessly.

He frowned slightly. 'How d'you mean, dear? What's happened where?'

'What's going on in chambers? What are the police doing? Please, you've got to tell me.'

'There's been an unfortunate incident and the police are making the usual kind of inquiries. There's absolutely no need to worry, my pet.'

'But what kind of incident?'

'Traynton found a dead man in my room this morning.'

'Radwick, please come home to lunch. You must come back.'

'But I've a great deal of work ...'

'Never mind that. You've got to come.' There was a short pause and when she spoke again her voice was calmer. 'I want you here so much, darling, so that I can ... can apologise for being funny last night.'

He tapped the desk with his fingers. He preferred not to be reminded about last night when his wife had, quite out of the blue, acted as if he were a leper. It was not as though he were always making demands on her, like some men did: nor did it as often go wrong because he was tired as she had tried to make out. Still, if she realized now that she had been overwrought and wanted to apologize ...

'You will come, my darling, won't you?' she said softly, before cutting the connection.

He replaced the receiver.

'I won't keep you a couple of minutes more, sir,' said Brock.

'What makes you think you're going to keep me at all?' he answered, as he wondered what kind of a mood she'd be in when he arrived home.

'I'm sure you'll just help us. Squire, get the stuff ready, will you?'

Squire, who had been standing throughout the meeting, opened the small plastic zip case he had been carrying and took from it a tube that looked very much like a large toothpaste tube, together with several paper handkerchiefs. He put the tube on the desk. 'Shove it on as if it were handcream,' he said.

'I do not use handcream,' snapped Holter.

Brock stood up, picked up the tube and unscrewed the top. He walked round to the right of Holter. 'Just put your hands out, will you?' Holter looked as though he might refuse, but then he slowly did as requested. Brock squeezed out a wavy six inch line of light green jelly on to Holter's right hand. 'If you'll work it very well in, sir.'

Holter rubbed his hands together.

Brock continued speaking. 'I wonder if you've any idea of the time when you and Mr Corry left these chambers last night, sir?'

'A little after six. I can't give it any more exactly than that.'

'And you went home?'

'No, I didn't. I was speaking at the CA Harper society dinner on the hidden dangers of delegated legislation and extra-judicial courts.'

'But I suppose you went straight to wherever the dinner was held?' Brock watched the jelly on Holter's hands. It had not changed colour.

'It was at The Three Bells and the quality of the meal was so bad that if I'd been running the society I would have complained most strongly. No, I did not go straight there. I went for a walk in the public gardens to consider the implications of my consultation with Corry. Would you also like to know how many times I blew my nose between then and going to bed?'

'You can tell me if you like, sir. It might come in handy.' Brock turned and spoke to the detective constable. 'Squire, pass Mr Holter a couple of those paper handkerchiefs so he can wipe the muck off.'

The handkerchiefs were given to him and Holter cleaned his hands. 'Are you satisfied my hands are now not only clean, but clear?' he asked, with forced sarcasm.

'Quite satisfied, sir.' Then Brock added, as if an amused afterthought: 'Though if you had fired the gun and then washed your hands several times, especially with a detergent, we wouldn't find any trace now.'

Holter picked up his brief.

Brock spoke casually. 'When was the last time you had a lady in your room, sir?'

'What the devil d'you mean by that?'

'Nothing suggestive.'

'I have no idea.'

'Would it be recently?'

'No.'

'Just one more small point. How did you get that bruise on your neck?'

Holter flushed. 'Mind your own bloody business,' he snapped, as he marched out of the room.

Brock yawned. 'Let's go, Squire. I wouldn't say no, myself, to a bite at the local.'

Squire scrumpled up the two used paper handkerchiefs and threw them into the half-full waste-paper basket. 'Someone told me he was a ripe old bastard. Now I know they weren't exaggerating.'

'His description lies in the eyes of his beholders. Some of the old lags he's got off wouldn't agree with you.' As Brock yawned again and stretched, his well worn coat strained at the shoulders. 'I wonder why his wife's so worried?'

* * *

Holter drove at eighty on the main road and slowed to sixty in the lanes, where forty was the maximum safe speed. He liked the country without ever suffering the land hunger which always attacked a real countryman. He lived out of Hertonhurst because that was a smarter thing to do than to live in the town, which was being ruined by speculative building.

As he drove through the village of Crighton, he raised a hand in a quick wave to the local publican, then almost immediately did the same to the rotund farmer from whom they bought all their cream. Although he would never have admitted it even to himself, he liked to think he was the squire, driving through his village. Sometimes, as the Bentley purred past the local villagers, he deliberately recalled how his father, before the First World War, had touched his forelock to the doctor, the parson, and the gentry from the big house.

He reached the drive of Treybrake Hall and turned into it. The gardener, mowing the front lawn, ignored the car completely, not even pausing to look at it. He was a surly man whom Holter would have sacked some time ago if there had been the chance of replacing him, but good gardeners were just as scarce here as everywhere else. The garden was a large one and Holter liked to open it to the public twice a year in aid of the Distressed Gentlefolk's Aid Association: without a gardener he would never have done this because he would have been ashamed had anything been less than perfect.

He parked in front of the massive porch and went through the open doorway into the house. Agnes Utley, a woman of fifty who came every week-day to do the housework, wished him good morning as she walked out of the dining-room. He asked her where Mrs Holter was and she told him in the drawing-room.

The drawing-room, to the right of the hall, was the best room from which to look at the view. The land, mostly woods, sloped down to the Romney Marsh and a headland cut out the obscene super-pylons which had been built without any regard for natural beauty. In spring, one could see the bulb-growing areas which became distant patchworks of colours.

Holter had commissioned a very well known interior decorator to decorate the house. This man was extremely precious by nature and he prided himself on being very, very expressive in his work. Ignoring the obvious, which was to treat the house with a traditional reverence and so enhance the beautiful Queen Anne architecture, he had throughout made use of brilliant and contrasting colours. The drawing-room looked as if it had been splattered by a exploding box of paints.

Holter found Charlotte drinking, which irritated him because of his old-fashioned and irrational dislike of seeing people drink on their own. 'Now what's all the trouble, Betty?'

She looked at him, her boldly made-up and beautiful

face showing signs of worry and strain. 'Radwick, I've been so worried.'

He crossed to the cocktail cabinet and poured himself out a whisky and soda. 'Why?'

'Please, Radwick, come and sit down here with me on the sofa so that I can be near you.'

He had intended to be pleasant but somewhat distant, thereby showing how hurt he had been by her behaviour the previous night. Now, however, as he looked at her, leaning forward so that her low cut dress fell open, he was swept by a familiar emotion and longing which set up a thumping at the base of his neck and dried his mouth. He sat down on the settee.

She took hold of his free hand in hers. 'Oh, Raddy, without you here to help me I've been all weepy.'

He drank quickly. Just the touch of her hand filled his mind with aching desires. He silently cursed her for having this effect and robbing him of his anger.

'Radwick, darling. I've been desperate to say how sorry I was for last night. I know I got cross with you, and it was all my fault.'

'It doesn't matter.'

'But it does matter, most desperately. I was so terribly tired. Can you forgive me, Radwick? Will you forgive me?' She leaned against him and kissed his neck, using her tongue, then whispered: 'I've been nearly out of my mind with worry. Someone told me something terrible had happened at your chambers and I kept thinking it might be you and that made me hysterical. My love, I can't even think of you cutting your finger without feeling as if I'd been twisted up inside.'

'You silly. You mustn't be like that.'

She moved even closer to him, after bringing his right arm round her waist. To him, it was pure chance that his right hand cupped her breast. 'What's happened?' she asked.

Her breast filled his hand. When he spoke, his voice was thick. 'A man called Corry was found dead in my room. He'd been shot.' He drank.

'But who's Corry?'

'A solicitor.'

'Oh, Radwick, suppose it had been you! Thank goodness I don't know him – that would have been so terrible.'

'You've met him. Tall and broad shouldered and over-polite to all ladies.'

'I'm sure I've never met him.'

'Of course you have. I had to intoduce you to him at Mrs Topham's cocktail party. You said afterwards that he was so smooth he reminded you of a snake.'

'I ... Yes, now I think I do remember him. But how did he get shot in your room?'

'The police haven't any idea.'

'I suppose it was an accident?'

'It must have been,' he answered uncertainly, remembering certain circumstances which seemed to militate against such a solution. His voice quickened. 'Whatever it was, he's made a blasted nuisance of himself. Police all over the place, not allowed into my own room, and that's when I've enough work for six men.'

'Was there ... Do the police think anyone was with him at the time?'

'Damned if I know.'

'The police haven't said anything?'

'Nothing other than an impertinent question as to when I last had a woman in my room.' He felt her start. 'What's the matter, love?'

'I've just been bitten by something.'

'Where?'

'Right up on my leg.' She drew up her skirt. 'Can you see anything?'

He pretended to look and after a few seconds she giggled. 'Darling, you're much too hungry! No, Radwick, you mustn't, or I shan't be in a fit state to eat anything. You're as bad as a boy of twenty.' Very gently, she drew his hand away and replaced her skirt.

He finished his drink. It was amusing, now, to remember what Brendon Feeney had said to him just before his marriage to Charlotte. Brendon was the first friend he had made after coming south to Hertonhurst. Brendon, embarrassed but determined to say what he thought he ought to, had talked wildly about the dangers of a man of fifty four marrying a girl of twenty-two. Brendon had repeated all the ancient, traditional, and ridiculous objections to such a disparity of ages and had finally gone so far as to suggest that although he was getting married with his eyes shut, Charlotte's were wide open and firmly fixed on his income. Brendon and he had hardly spoken to each other since then and now he was sorry for that because he would have liked to ask Brendon whether the success of a marriage between different age-groups didn't obviously depend on the people concerned and not on a whole series of platitudinous objections. He loved Charlotte and she so clearly loved him just as passionately. Their age difference meant nothing, had no significance. She had married him because of what he was and not for his wealth. To be utterly frank, there had been times when there was some slight temporary trouble between them, but what marriage escaped these trivia no matter what were the partners' ages?

'A penny for your thoughts?' she whispered.

'How very, very much I love you.'

'Radwick, you're so wonderful to me, even though all I seem to be able to do is to behave like last night. But I was so tired and I had a headache and when you kept wanting to play ding-a-ling I lost my temper. I kept hating myself this morning when I remembered how I'd hit you. Did I hurt you?'

'Of course not.'

'But there's a bruise on your neck. I'm going to kiss it to take all the hurt away. Radwick, please never, never let me go. I couldn't bear to be without you.'

A surge of deep emotion made his eyes prickle. He had found perfect success both in his career and his marriage. No man could ask for more than he had.

'Tell me exactly how much you love me, Radwick?'

There was a knock on the door and they drew apart. She adjusted her dress. 'Yes?' she called out.

'Lunch is ready,' said Agnes Utley from outside.

'Thank you.' Charlotte lowered her voice. 'D'you forgive me, Radwick?'

'For anything and everything.'

They stood up.

She put her arm round his waist, or as far round his

comfortable middle-aged waist as she could reach. 'Darling ...' She hesitated, then finished speaking with a rush of words. 'Why did the police ask you when a woman had last been in your room in chambers?'

'I've no idea,' he replied uninterestedly.

Chapter Six

WHILE UNIFORMED men and two detective constables inquired into Corry's home life, Brock returned to chambers after a quick lunch at the nearest public house in the High Street. He never liked to be far away from the scene of the crime at the beginning of investigations because he tried, as he put it, to soak up the atmosphere, the circumstances, and the personalities. A lecturing detective superintendent at Kirkton College, where he had taken the sergeant's course, had said: 'All crimes are governed by personalities.' As with all generalisations, this was far too facile a simplification, but even so, there was a great deal of truth in it. He thought about the personalities as he at present saw them – Holter, so very sure of himself in most ways but probably unsure of himself when he considered his standing in the world, bombastic, impatient with others, apparently unconcerned with the tragedy of a murder: Resse, coldly cynical even with regard to himself: Aiden, an exuberant, extrovert young man: Traynton, a ponderous, but immensely self-satisfied refugee from a bygone age: Marriott, too smartly smart, contemptuous of anything but financial success: and Joan Fleming, every ready to say she was married, as if not to spread temptation before others. Those, and Spender who was away for the day, were the personalities in the case.

He crossed the road and walked into Awcott House. At the head of the stairs were three reporters who surrounded him and demanded a statement and he replied that as soon as possible a news conference would be called, but until then nothing could be said. He refused their continued pleas for some form of concrete news, but did so in a way that left them bearing him no ill will.

He entered chambers and went through to the clerks' room. Only Marriott was there.

'It's a warm day,' said Brock, as he moved one of the wooden chairs and sat down on it. He looked up at the dusty photographs on the wall of men in full-bottom wigs. 'When it gets this warm I have difficulty in thinking of anything but cool seas and bikinis.'

'You go for bikinis, do you?' replied Marriott, as he stubbed out the cigarette he had been smoking.

'Show me the man who doesn't and I'll prescribe a psychiatrist,' replied Brock equably. 'When's Mr Spender due back?'

'He might look in tonight, or he might not.'

'Someone said he's on a case?'

'We're defending a man who crashed into a stationary police car.'

'Now there's a damn' silly thing to do! Is Spender a nice bloke?'

Marriott picked up a packet of cigarettes and, after a slight pause, offered it before helping himself to one. 'He's all right. Makes more money than Mr Resse, anyway.'

Brock struck a match and leaned forward to offer the light. 'Yet Resse is the older man. I'd have thought he was doing quite well?'

'Him?' Marriott spoke scornfully. 'He'd make a better living driving the corporation dust-cart. I'll tell you straight, his briefs come in here marked in fives and sevens. A man like him ought to be getting near the hundreds as often as not. He's no bloody good in court. I could do better than he does.'

'I wonder you haven't tried, then?'

Marriott looked quickly at the detective, but seeing only the same bland expression he took no notice of the remark. 'He got a lot of work from Corry.'

'Did he?'

'But Corry didn't like paying up what was owing. Did you know that a barrister can't sue a solicitor for his fees?'

'No, I didn't.'

'It's some goddamn, stupid rule from the Middle Ages, like the rest of the law. Corry owed him something well over two hundred quid and Mr Resse was always on to Old Misery – that's Traynton – to try to shake it out of Corry.'

'But he didn't succeed?'

'Not recently. As a matter of fact ...' Marriott trailed off into silence.

'Yes?'

'I might be speaking out of turn.'

'I can't tell you whether you are until you've said what you're going to say.'

The telephone rang and Marriott answered the call. After a minute, he put the receiver on the desk and stood up. 'Papers are missing. Papers are always missing. Goddamn' world couldn't turn round without 'em.' He walked over to the mantelpiece and searched amongst the briefs that were there and found what he wanted. He returned to the telephone and told the caller that the Request for Further and Better Particulars would be delivered that day.

Brock spoke once the call was over. 'You were going to say something?'

'Was I?'

'You were.'

'Well. Like I said, I don't want to cause trouble, but ... Well, Corry was with Mr Resse before he went in to see Mr Holter. I went past the room and there wasn't half a row going on.'

'Thanks for telling me. These things often mean nothing, but they do help us to sort out the facts.' Brock flicked the ash from his cigarette into the ash-tray.

Marriott brought a penknife out of his coat pocket, opened out the small blade, and began to pare his nails. Brock hastily looked away before he spoke again. 'I don't think I've checked with you about last night?'

'No.'

'Now's as good a time as any to get it over and done with. What time did you leave here?'

'Some time after five-thirty. It should be five-thirty sharp, but Old Misery belly-aches if I don't hang on a bit.'

'D'you go straight home?'

'Yes.'

'Not married, are you?'

'Too smart for that. Love 'em, I says, and then leave 'em bloody quickly.'

'Live with your parents?'

'That's right.'

'Well, that's fine.' Brock judged from the cessation of sound that Marriott had finished with his nails.

The door opened and Traynton entered. He stared with patent dislike at the detective, turned and hung his bowler hat on one of the hooks of the mahogany stand.

'Just one more question,' said Brock, as he stood up. 'Looking at them in a lump, would you call the people in these chambers successful?'

Traynton forestalled what Marriott had been going to say. 'We should not presume to pass an opinion on such a matter.'

As Brock left the room, he was smiling.

Traynton went over to his desk. He stared at Marriott. 'I trust you told that man nothing of any importance?'

'You know me. I keep my mouth shut tighter than a bleeding clam.'

'I have asked you before not to use that kind of language. It is neither seemly nor fitting to chambers.'

'Yeah? Then what d'you call a bloke who's head's been half shot off?'

For once, Traynton was without an answer.

*   *   *

Resse walked slowly back along the High Street after eating lunch at the corner café. As he came abreast of an electrical store, he stopped. A sale was on and a twin-tub washing machine was offered for ten pounds less than usual. He sighed as he scratched his rather beaky nose. For years he had promised himself he would buy a washing machine for his wife and for years he had been unable to.

As he stood there, the sunlight warming the back of his neck, he wondered what Georgina thought about their marriage in the secret part of her mind. She came from a county family who, until the Second World War, had had a large estate. Her father, brothers, uncles, and cousins, had been Lord Lieutenants and MFHs, they had shot partridges by the hundreds and pheasants by the thousands, they had known beyond doubt they were the chosen. After the war, they were, by their standards, relatively poor and without power, but they were still the county. As such, they only warmly recognised county or success.

He was a failure. Failure was one of those words which only found meaning by comparisons. Compared with a clerk stifled in some ugly London skyscraper office block, he was successful: compared with Holter, he was a failure. Georgina made light of his failure to reach the position he should have done, but he sometimes saw her look at him with a wondering, perplexed expression.

He turned away from the shop. Bitterly, he remembered how Holter had recently mentioned that Charlotte had bought the latest Bendix which did everything but fold up the clothes and hand them over. Charlotte would always have the latest, biggest, and most expensive. Without any natural taste, she correlated price with quality. Suddenly, Resse smiled sarcastically. Here he was, criticizing her for judging the world by the money it cost when a second ago he had judged his own life by the money he made.

He walked down the High Street to chambers and passed a small knot of onlookers who were blocking half the pavement. As he went up the short path to the doorway, he heard the murmur of several people all talking at once. Whom had they identified him as? Detective, pathologist, reporter, undertaker ... ?

There were five reporters waiting at the head of the stairs. They crowded round him and asked him what was going on. He said that the dead man had sat up and asked for a couple of aspirins. He knocked on the door and the uniformed policeman inside opened it for him. His last view of the reporters was of their worried expressions, as if they were wondering whether they were missing a resurrection.

He went along to his room. Aiden was sitting at the smaller desk, reading an American edition of *Fanny Hill*.

'I see you're very busy,' observed Resse, as he sat down.

'Why aren't there women like her around these days?'

'There are, but they're called whores and never, never allowed to live happily ever after. That's the new morality.'

'You make it all sound so depressing.'

'I've defended any number of prostitutes on any number of charges. With one notable exception, they were extremely depressing.'

'Let's talk about the exception.'

'Her name was Helen. She could easily have been the daughter of Leda.'

'Come again?'

'Can you really be that ignorant, Gregory?'

'Only if I try hard.'

Resse lit a cigarette, careless that he was exceeding his normal consumption, a figure dictated by finances. 'Have you finished that Reply?'

Aiden reluctantly put the book down. 'I've tried twice, without success. I've decided my forte is not going to be pleading, but sheer downright brilliant advocacy.'

'What makes you think you'll have a forte?'

'Well, I can't be hopeless at everything.'

There was a quick knock on the door and Brock looked into the room. 'May I come in, gentlemen?'

'Surely the question is, can we refuse you?' retorted Resse.

Brock stepped inside. 'Since coming to these chambers, sir, I'm not quite certain what I can do and what I can't. On the one hand there's Mr Holter, ever ready to correct me, and on the other there's Mr Traynton, aching to see me charged with something horrid.'

'Scylla and Charybdis.'

'I beg your pardon, sir?'

'I'm not the only one,' said Aiden.

Brock looked questioningly at him, but when nothing more was said he turned and asked Resse: 'I wondered if I might have a word or two with you, sir?'

'I thought I was declared honest after that jelly you put on my hands failed to change colour?'

'It's just a matter of routine, sir.'

'The most alarming answer of all. Last year I had a case,

Inspector, in which I defended a man charged with indecently assaulting a girl of seven. During his arrest by two six foot tall policemen he suffered very extensive bruising and lost three teeth. The policemen insisted on calling it a routine arrest.'

'Maybe they had daughters, sir.'

'Sometime, Inspector, I'd like to discuss with you the proposition that as the benefits of civilisation increase, so does the need for reversion to the *lex talionis*.'

'Some time, sir, but right now I want to talk about something else.'

'Are you tactfully suggesting my pupil should absent himself?'

'I think it would be better.'

'Gregory,' said Resse, 'can you find yourself gainful occupation in some other room? For want of anything else, you might attempt, once more, to formulate that Reply.'

'I'll try,' promised Aiden, as he stood up. He took the book with him.

'Take a seat, Inspector,' said Resse.

'Thanks,' replied Brock, as he sat down. 'I was wondering it you could tell me a little about what kind of man the dead man was?'

'I can certainly tell you little if you want me to be complimentary, but I can become quite loquacious if you're willing to listen to the truth.'

Brock leaned aback in his chair, which creaked, and crossed his legs. 'No one seemed to have liked him very much.'

'That shows inherent good taste.'

'You sound as if you almost hated him?'

Resse stared at the detective, who was watching him with what appeared to be a sleepy expression. 'Hated him enough to shoot him?'

'I didn't say so.'

'Inspector, someone who didn't know I was in earshot once described me as a man of feverish cerebral activity but almost complete physical immobility. However much I hated and despised Corry, and however often I murdered him in my mind, I would never have actually shot him.'

'You're surprisingly harsh on yourself, sir.'

'Let me thank you for the implied compliment. You have cause to praise Resse, but not to bury him.'

Brock produced a packet of cigarettes and offered it. Resse accepted one. Brock asked if it would be all right if he took off his coat.

'By all means, just so long as you're not wearing braces. I'm afraid I have a thing about braces which show.'

'Too much like 'Appy 'Ampstead? Now, sir, I believe you had a row with the dead man yesterday afternoon?'

Resse started heavily. He went to smoke, noticed his hand was trembling and dropped it on to his lap.

'Is that true?' asked Brock, in the same friendly voice.

'News travels fast, but bad news travels a damn' sight faster.'

'What was the row about?'

Very carefully, trying to keep his hand steady, Resse raised the cigarette and smoked. 'How much have you learned about Corry's character?' he asked, at length.

'Suppose you save time and tell me your estimate of it?'

Resse stared down at the top of his desk. 'He was born on the Marsh. His people were small tradesmen and he never stopped feeling he ought to be ashamed because of it. He envied anyone he considered better than himself and despised anyone he knew to be worse, and in this context education and background were the determining factors. He was the kind of anarchistic and anachronistic snob I hope my few words have led you to expect: he'd rush to be seen chatting to a "name" and then afterwards think up a hundred and one reasons for being scornful of the man. He detested the Establishment and yet would have given almost anything to have belonged to it. He knew money could never buy him acceptance into the kind of society he wanted to join, yet he perversely tried to use money to get there. One thing, Inspector, you must realize that I use the term "society" very loosely. This part of Kent is noted not for its apples, cherries, hops, and women, but for the forty thieves of Hertonhurst, the venality of certain of the town officials, and the two genuine aristocrats who have the sense to live most of the time somewhere else.'

'You seem to have studied him closely, sir?'

'Know thine enemy.'

'Then you considered him your enemy?'

'I ... I should have remembered to guard my tongue.' Resse was silent for several seconds, but then he suffered the compulsion to speak. 'What is it now? The solemn declaration and warning that I needn't say anything, but anything I may say will be taken down and may be used in evidence?'

'I didn't think we'd reached that point. Having told me a bit about Corry, sir, perhaps you'll go back to the row you had with him?'

'How do you define "row"?'

'By using a measure of common-sense.'

Resse stubbed out his cigarette. 'I had an argument with him. It wasn't the first, but it's clearly the last.'

'What about?'

'Money. What else do people argue about?'

'Was it the money he owed you, but wouldn't pay?'

Resse stood up, pushed his chair back, and paced the floor. 'So it's every man for himself?'

'I don't follow you.'

'Obviously, someone in chambers has supplied news both about the row and its cause. Why not? As French seamen shout at the first opportunity, *sauve qui peut*. Corry owed me something between two hundred and three hundred quid, money clients had paid him for my work and which he was holding on to. I couldn't sue him for it. In the first place, I'm not allowed to, in the second, who kills the goose which lays the golden egg — even if the gold is somewhat tarnished? He amused himself by releasing the money in dribs and drabs, knowing how much I needed the whole lot. He used to give me a great deal of work, but marked it low, knowing I couldn't afford to refuse it. Yesterday afternoon he came to see Holter about a case and I found him waiting in the clerks' room. I asked him into here and said I must have some of the money. He asked me why I was so impatient. I lost my temper. It happens even to the most psychologically adjusted amongst us.'

'I supposed something caused the ill feeling between you right at the beginning?'

'Our respective wives. Men are so much better at hiding their dislikes than women are. Corry's wife — she left him several years ago – was as objectionable in her way as he is ... was ... in his. She mistook my wife's attitude for snobbishness when in fact it was no more than ordinary dislike.'

Brock smiled momentarily. 'I suppose you can say there was one good result of your wives' quarrel. In order to lord it over you, he gave you briefs.'

'You're suggesting that but for his hatred of my wife and me, he would have briefed a more competent barrister?'

'I said nothing of the sort, sir.'

'Didn't you? Then you thought it.'

Brock scratched the top of his head at a point where his hair was very thin. 'Was the row a long one?'

'I still maintain "row" is the wrong word since that takes two and he held both aces and trumps.'

'How long did it last, sir?'

'Corry left this room when word arrived that Holter was ready to see him. Holter could afford the pleasure of deciding when he was ready.'

'And was that the end?'

Resse stopped pacing the floor, hesitated, and sat down. 'I did not see him again in the evening, I did not lose my temper for a second time, and I did not finish off his worthless life with one well aimed bullet.'

'Then I wonder if you'd fill in what you were doing last night between leaving here and arriving at home?'

'Suppose you tell me the time of death?'

'We don't know it yet.'

'Don't know, or won't tell so that I have to try and cover myself for the whole evening? I left here before six and I must have arrived home a little after quarter past seven.'

'Did you drive home?'

'No, Inspector. Walking is not so quick, but it's far cheaper.'

'The walk can't have taken you over an hour and a quarter?'

'On the way, I called in at a public house and treated myself to two half-pints of bitter which I couldn't afford. Whilst I drank them, I dwelt on the pleasures of subjecting Corry to *peine forte et dure*.'

'Or of shooting him?'

'Far too quick.'
'Which pub was this?'
'The Horsemen of Harlech.'
'They're sure to remember you?'
'I doubt it. The place was full of tired businessmen on their way home to their ten thousand pound houses.'
Brock stood up. He picked up his coat from the back of the chair and folded it over his left arm. 'Thanks very much.'
'No handcuffs for me?'
'I never carry them around. They wear out the pockets too quickly.'
Resse fiddled with a pencil. He did not speak until Brock's right hand was on the handle of the door. 'Is it certain it wasn't suicide?'
'Not yet.'
'But you wouldn't rate the chances very high?'
'Lower than a snake's belly.' Brock left the room.
Resse dropped the pencil on to the desk.

Chapter Seven

ON HIS return to the main police station, in Whitaker Road, Brock made a quick report to the divisional superintendent and then went along to his own room. As he stepped inside, he vaguely noticed that it was untidy.

He sat down at his desk and stared at the papers on it. He hated paperwork and tried to leave it on one side and forget it, but HQ were always shouting for this form or that one. He thought about his chances of promotion to detective chief inspector. The Corry case could make or break that chance. Murders were always difficult for the police because the public believed them to be a crime apart and as such they received maximum publicity. Success meant publicized success, failure meant publicized failure. A less ambitious man than himself might have suggested to the chief constable that as an insurance and because of the standing of the people concerned, Scotland Yard's murder squad be called in.

He thought about Resse. An embittered man, yet not wholly bitter, who had the strongest of motives for killing Corry, hatred.

The telephone rang. The call was from the detective superintendent at HQ to say he was coming down from Maidstone to check how the case was going. Brock managed to sound as if he would welcome the visit.

Almost as he replaced the receiver, there was a knock on the door and Detective Constable Yawley entered. Yawley, a man in middle age, had been a DC for 15 years and would retire a DC. ' 'Evening sir,' he said.

' 'Evening,' answered Brock automatically, and when he looked at his watch he was surprised to discover the time was almost six o'clock.

'I've made inquiries at Corry's office, sir,' said Yawley, in his toneless voice. 'The people there don't seem to have liked him very much.'

'He was pushing hard for the title of the world's least liked resident. Have you discovered any sort of connection outside work between him and anyone in chambers?'

'No, sir. I gather he never mixed with anyone but the woman.'

'What woman?'

'There is a woman who frequently visits his house at night.'

'You're saying she's no lady?' Brock smiled. Yawley belonged to some obscure religious sect which held that almost everything in the world was sinful. 'See her and have a talk.'

'Very well, sir,' replied Yawley, stiffly.

'D'you know where she lives?'

'No, sir. I did not pursue the matter.'

'Then start pursuing. See if she can tell you anything about Corry's other love lives.'

Yawley left. Brock lit a cigarette and thought that Yawley must find the present world a very depressing place.

The telephone rang. Kinnet, the Home Office pathologist who had conducted the PM, wanted to talk about the case. Would the DI be able to drop in to see him at his home and enjoy a glass?

After replacing the receiver, Brock stared at his full 'In' tray. He pushed it to one side of the desk, before getting up and leaving the room.

In the centre of the courtyard at the back of the station were two black police cars, clean and polished, and his own eight-year-old Hillman which was rusting and had not had a polish in months. He climbed into his car and made a note of the mileage in the log book from which his mileage allowance was calculated. He drove out of the courtyard.

Kinnet, one of the six pathologists in the south-east, lived on the northern outskirts of Hertonhurst. He owned a large, comfortable house, set in an attractive garden, the kind of house Brock would have liked but would never be able to afford.

Kinnet opened the front door. He was a tall, thin, stooping Scotsman, with a brusque manner which frequently upset people inclined to pompousness. ''Evening, Brock,' he said, as he shook hands. 'Good of you to come out here. Let's go in my study where we shan't be disturbed.' He pushed the door open and Brock went into a room which was furnished for comfort rather than style. 'What will you drink?'

'Whisky, please.'

'You'll have to take it with water, mind, not soda. I have it sent down from the Moal distillery in Angus and I'll no' have anyone ruining it with bubbles. If you find the taste is unusual that's because there's a decent amount of honest to God malt whisky in it.'

After he had poured out the drinks, Kinnet stood with his back to the empty fireplace. 'Did you know Corry?'

'No, I didn't.'

'Not my idea of company, but people used to say he was a clever lawyer.'

'He was sharp.'

'And no honest policeman likes a sharp lawyer, of course?' Kinnet drank slowly, savouring the flavour of the whisky. He put the glass on the mantelpiece. 'You can rule out suicide, Brock. The chances of suicide are about one in a million and those are the figures I'll give in the witness-box. You can have the reasons very succinctly. There's no note nor any history of attempted or threatened suicide: people do commit suicide first time without leaving notes, but one can say it's unusual. No powder markings on Corry's hands. Not a very satisfactory negative, since the murder gun can be fired without leaving appreciable deposits on the hand and the test to uncover such deposits isn't very much more reliable with the new jelly stuff than it was with the old paraffin test. Still, it's a straw in the wind.

'In order to find how far from the body the gun was when it was fired, I borrowed the corpse of an old tramp. I shot eight bullets into the corpse, using ammunition identical with that used to kill Corry. As you know, there's a difference between the tattooing of power-blackening on live, warm flesh and on dead, cold flesh, but the margin of error in distance isn't much above five per cent. I can say beyond any shadow of doubt that the gun was fired at a minimum distance of fifteen inches from the man's head. Practically no suicide holds a gun as much as an inch away from his flesh for very obvious reasons.

'The gun has a most unusual safety catch which really is difficult to find and being in a hurry I had to ring up the man in ballistics before I could sort out how it worked. You'll see what I mean when you get his report. They say the gun at one time must have been used for target practice by someone who did his own modifications. Like all four five five Webleys, it's got a double action and because of the safety catch which had replaced one of the side screws and has altered the action, the pull on the trigger, if the gun isn't cocked, has to be several times greater than usual: so much so that it's very difficult to fire. If the gun's cocked it becomes a hair trigger action, but the safety catch automatically engages.'

Brock twisted the glass in his hands. 'Corry, then, could hardly have pulled the trigger by mistake unless he cocked the gun and if he did cock it he probably wouldn't have been able to fire it for quite a time because he'd be looking for the safety catch?'

'The ballistics report puts the thing accurately, but I'd say that's a correct summing up.'

'Then the gun, on its own, rules out accident?'

'That's not my department, Inspector, but as a man who prides himself on ordinary intelligence I could not be convinced of accident in the light of those facts.'

Brock drank. He thought about the face powder – he was certain that was what it was – that had been on the carpet of Holter's room in chambers. 'Had Corry been in any sort of a scuffle?'

'The only bruise on his whole body came from falling to the floor.'

'What about the trail on the carpet – was it blood?'

'Blood, human, Corry's.' Kinnet's voice quickened. 'There's a nice bit of research here, Inspector, that's wasted at the moment. The lab boys have grouped the blood down to show an LV a plus b factor which is probably possessed by only one person in every million.'

'Did he crawl or was he pulled?'

'A nice question! I once had a man who walked and talked after a bullet had passed through both the frontal and temporal lobes of his brain. Still, in this case the bullet had begun to break up so that the damage was very great. I'm prepared to say that he died instantly, so that he was pulled across the floor.

'I did a nice bit of reconstruction of the shooting with bits of string and tape. When the gun was fired, Corry was looking away from it and the muzzle was one hundred and twenty degrees round from the horizontally projected line from between his eyes.' Kinnet took a pencil and held it at arm's length so that it was behind his ear, pointing at his head. 'This is the position, Inspector. There's no possibility of taking aim from here, which is just one more reason for the odds of a million to one against suicide.'

'Then you're confirming murder?'

'Aye. But did you really need confirmation?'

'No, not really.'

Kinnet finished his drink. He stepped away from the fireplace. 'You'll have the other half, Inspector? Two whiskies under the belt are better than one when it comes to making light of difficulties.' He took Brock's glass. 'How have you got on with the people in the case?'

'So-so,' replied Brock carefully.

'I've met Holter once or twice. He's not the kind of man I'd want to be stranded with on a desert island, but they say he's good in court. His wife's only half his age, isn't she?'

'Less than half, I think.'

'That always seems a damned silly situation, but I'm not certain there isn't a touch of wistful jealousy in my complaint! Who else is there with Holter?'

'Resse, Spender, and a young chap, Aiden, two clerks, and an occasional typist.'

'I know Resse. Quite a nice bloke when he allows himself to be: his wife's a real charmer.'

'I haven't met her yet.' Brock finished his whisky and stood up. 'I must push. My super said he was coming down from HQ so I'd better be around to greet him. Can you give me a time of death before I move, sir?'

'Somewhere between six and seven last night. You can take those times as accurate because he'd had sardines for lunch and it's been discovered that they have a very consistent rate of deterioration.'

'It's a nice job you've got, sir!'

'It's never been known to spoil my appetite,' replied Kinnet.

Brock left the house and drove towards the central police station. The traffic lights in the High Street were at red and as he waited, he thought about that trail of blood. If Corry was killed instantly, why had his body been dragged several feet along the carpet? To try to suggest suicide? How could it? And why had no further attempt been made to confuse the evidence?

* * *

Dectective Sergeant Peach waited in the lobby of The Three Bells and morosely stared at the loud-voiced, horse-faced woman who was talking to her ugly Pekinese as if it were a child. He hated dogs and he hated that kind of woman.

A man, dressed in a suit with a widely spaced and heavily

coloured check, came into the lobby. He was small and pugnaciously hail-fellow-well-met.

'Are you the copper wanting to know something?' he asked.

'I'm Detective Sergeant Peach of the county constabulary.'

'What's up? But you'll have to hurry. I've twenty-four special dinners, God knows how many coming to the dining-room, and one of the waitresses has just given notice.'

Peach silently applauded the good taste of the waitress. 'Can we go somewhere more private?'

'Charging me with something obscene? All right, let's use my office. But no more than five minutes. Bloody lobsters never came up from Folkestone this morning and I've had to change the entire menu for the specials.'

They went into a small room which was filled to capacity with a desk, chairs, three filing cabinets, a safe, and a mass of ledgers and papers.

'What's all the trouble?' asked the manager.

'You had the CA Harper Society dinner last night?'

'We did. A first-class mind-improving society and that's a fact. The mind's a sponge that starts life squeezed dry and even a lifetime of learning can't fill it right out. Most people don't begin even to dampen it.'

'Was Mr Holter the speaker?'

'Ah, ha! The murder! As I was saying to madam, my wife, not so many minutes ago, we may live in the country, but we do see life. Three weeks ago a rape in Ramsgate, two weeks ago a stabbing in Ashford, this week a murder in Hertonhurst. That's life for you.'

'No one's yet said it was murder.'

'No?' The manager was plainly disappointed.

'Have you any idea when Mr Holter arrived?'

'It was cocktails at six-thirty, dinner at seven. We like to dine early – I'm a member of the society – in order to leave plenty of time to enjoy the speaker's lecture afterwards. No man's mind can be too broadened.'

'When did he get here?'

'I was just telling you, old man. Cocktails at six thirty and dinner at seven. But our speaker never turned up at six-thirty and that's bad for trade because people get worried and don't drink up when the speaker's missing. Seven o'clock, no speaker, and dinner's waiting. Seven-five and already the food is suffering: seven-ten and the staff is asking me what on earth they're to do?'

'Put it back in the deep freeze for a bit?'

'That is not funny,' snapped the manager.

'When did he arrive?' asked Peach.

'At ten minutes past seven.'

'What state was he in? Calm?'

'Calm? No, sir, not calm, not by a jugful. He was in a state and no mistake. He demanded two drinks, even though the delicious food was spoiling.'

'What kind of a state?' asked Peach, and resentfully waited for a full description of the ruined meal before he obtained the information he wanted.

* * *

Holter, contrary to his normal habit and for no reason at all, drove home the back route, via the village of Wrasham. He had passed the general store when he noticed the Mercedes parked outside the call-box. Identifying it as his wife's car, he braked harshly and reversed the short distance, swerving violently. He climbed out and walked over to the call-box. As he reached the door, Charlotte saw his reflection in the mirror and was shocked.

He pulled open the door and held it open with his foot. 'Something wrong with the telephone at home, darling?'

She turned slowly. 'Wrong?' she muttered, and then hastily covered the mouthpiece of the receiver with her gloved hand.

'I suppose the damned thing's out of action for the second time this month? Here, let me tell them what I think of their service.' he held out his hand.

She pulled the receiver away from him. 'No.'

'The only way to get proper service these days is to speak up.'

She struggled to regain her self-control. 'I've ... I've told them, darling, so it's all right.' She replaced the receiver on its cradle and picked up her handbag from the top of the coin-box.

'D'you know, Betty, you really looked surprised to see me,' he said boisterously, as he held the door more fully open for her. 'As if I were the last person you expected to see. You thought your husband was miles away!'

She tucked her arm round his and interlaced three fingers.

'Of course I did, my darling, and I was talking to my favourite boy-friend and I didn't want anyone to hear.'

'You watch out, Madam, or I'll have him hauled up in court on every charge in the books.'

'It's such fun finding you're jealous.'

As they walked across the pavement, their bodies momentarily met at the hips and he thought he felt the ripple of her flesh as she moved her right leg forward. Not even a misogynist could deny she was beautiful, he thought. Men who saw her immediately envied her husband. It filled him with both a sense of pride and anger that at parties the men crowded round her and visually explored her body.

She squeezed his fingers and then withdrew her hand. 'I'll follow you back, but please don't drive too fast, darling. It terrifies me to think of something dreadful happening to you.'

He opened the driving door of the Mercedes for her and as she sat down her short skirt rode up her knees. 'Don't you ever get tired of looking?' she asked, smiling.

'Not until they nail me up in my coffin.'

He returned to the Bentley and started the engine. Thank God, even though he was fifty-eight, it still excited him to look at his wife's legs. And thank God he'd had the sense to wait for marriage to Charlotte – a woman who'd excite a man of fifty-eight or one hundred and eight.

Even though he drove as quickly as ever to Treybrake Hall, the Mercedes pulled up behind the Bentley in front of the house as he switched off the engine.

'Are you going out this evening?' he asked, as she stepped out of her car.

'Darling, I told you at breakfast. I'm having a fitting with Rachael. The woman who actually makes the clothes says she can't go any further until I have the fitting.'

'Aren't you ... seeing rather a lot of her?' he asked, trying to speak casually.

She smiled. 'Spoilsport! You're going out, so why shouldn't I?'

'Mine's business.'

'And mine's business. If I went to one of the London fashion houses instead of to Rachael's for my clothes, even you wouldn't be able to pay the bills. You know, underneath Rachael is really a very nice woman.'

'Underneath all those shapeless clothes, she probably looks as raddled as her face suggests.'

'You're very naughty about her and I'm sure you're only jealous of her?'

'Jealous?'

'You'd rather I sat at home and waited for you because you just don't like sharing me with anyone. I do so love you being like that, Radwick. It makes me feel all warm and important. You won't be back late tonight, will you?'

'Why?'

'Don't be so silly,' she whispered, 'I'm sure you've quite enough imagination to answer that one.' She spoke in her normal voice. 'I must go in and see that Mrs Utley's got the meal ready properly and not put the joint on the ring and the peas in the oven. She's stayed on to help as we're both going out.'

After she had gone inside, he turned and stared across the countryside at the distant horizon which was just visible through the shimmering heat haze that had lasted into the evening. He lit a cigarette. It was exciting to think about tonight. Tonight, he would be able to wash away memories that hurt: memories of the night before, when she had almost fought to keep him away from her bed. Women were irrational creatures, he tritely decided. As he looked across Romney Marsh, one or two of the broader dykes glinting in the sun, he suffered a sudden desire of possessiveness. He would have liked to own all the land before him so that he could deny anyone's entry into it, for the same reason that it was wonderful to know Charlotte was his, to the exclusion of every other man in the world.

He turned and went into the house. Charlotte was in the sitting-room and when he suggested a drink she said she would like a whisky and would he give Mrs Utley a small gin to help try to keep her in a good humour. Charlotte left to go into the kitchen and he poured out the three drinks and put the glasses on to a silver tray. He went into the hall and was about to walk to the kitchen when he looked at the telephone and was reminded that Charlotte had said it was out of order. He put the tray down and picked up the receiver. The dialling tone sounded immediately. He dialled nought and when the operator answered he explained he was checking the circuit.

In the kitchen, Charlotte was preparing the salad and Mrs Utley, looking uglier than ever, was whipping some cream. He put the tray down on the central table. 'I've just checked the telephone and it's all right now,' he said. 'For once, they corrected the fault quickly.'

'There's never been nothing wrong with that,' said Mrs Utley, in her harsh voice. 'Been ringing all night. Never no time to see to the meal, there hasn't been.'

'It wasn't working just now,' said Charlotte hurriedly. 'That's why I had to go out and report it.'

Mrs Utely stopped beating the cream. 'Been going all the time. Someone ringed you whilst you was out, but wouldn't say who she was.'

'I tell you, it wasn't working.' Charlotte's voice was high pitched.

'What's it matter?' said Holter, as he picked up the glass filled with whisky and soda and handed it to his wife.

Chapter Eight

AFTER A LARGE breakfast, his wife did not believe in diets, Brock left home and drove through the back streets of Hertonhurst to the central police station. As he arrived, the superintendent was stepping out of his car. The superintendent, pedantic and cautious as ever, insisted on an immediate report and it was a quarter of an hour before

Brock managed to escape and go to his own room. After shutting the door, he took off his coat. The weather had been so hot for so many days now that his mind seemed haunted by memories of a little cottage in the one part of Cornwall that trippers had not yet ruined.

The report from ballistics was on his desk and he read it through. The revolver and its unusual action were described in great technical detail. It was confirmed that the bullet dug out of the bookcase had been fired from the .455 Webley in question.

Brock leaned back in his chair. The trail of blood worried him. Why in the hell had the dead Corry been dragged from near the display cabinet to the desk? Every explanation that occurred to him proved, on examination, to be obviously defective. He shook his head and leaned forward and began to read through the mail. Requests for witness statements, circulars from HQ admonishing, advising, and correcting, lists of stolen cars and stolen property, lists from local magistrates' courts detailing the days for hearings, advertising circulars, and finally one typewritten, anonymous letter.

'Wot about Mrs Holter's boy-friend and wot about Spender's car accident? They ain't so lily-white as they looks.'

Brock lit a cigarette. The style of the letter suggested a writer who thought that mis-spellings and some fractured grammar automatically made the writer out to be an illiterate.

* * *

Alan Spender, looking because of his unlined face and tight curly hair younger than thirty-seven, parked his Rapier, locked it, walked to the end of the road and into the High Street. Outside chambers was one bored reporter who asked him if he knew what was going on and accepted, without any display of emotion, that he had no idea. He went through to the clerks' room.

'Good morning, sir,' said Traynton.

''Morning, sir,' said Marriott. 'Lovely day for a holiday.' Marriott admired Spender because he was successful.

Spender took a brief out of his case and handed it to

Traynton. 'There you are, Josephus, all duly signed, sealed, and delivered.'

'How did we do, sir?'

'We were found guilty, fined fifty quid, and licence endorsed for a year. The police were definitely feeling slightly vindictive about their nice new car. My story was heart-breakingly sincere, but it suffered the disadvantage of being disbelieved.'

'Mr Seabord was on the phone, sir,' said Marriott, 'and he ...'

'I can inform Mr Spender of the substance of the communication,' cut in Traynton loudly.

'What the hell's it matter who tells him?'

Traynton sniffed loudly. 'I hesitate to think about what will go on in these chambers once I have left them.'

Spender grinned. 'Never mind the internecine strife. What did the old crook, Seabord, want?'

'He has briefed you in the High Court, sir,' said Traynton. 'A case of breach of contract.'

'Good for him. His firm's really been pulling their collective fingers out.'

'I must admit there has been a satisfactory amount of work from them in the past year, sir. They used, of course, to brief Mr Pace until he took Silk. I hope that they now regard you as a suitable junior.'

'Push up the fees, Josephus. Nothing under a hundred guineas.' Spender sat down on Traynton's desk.'What the hell's got into chambers with Corry getting himself shot?'

'A most unpleasant happening, sir,' said Traynton.

'Was he murdered?'

'Unofficially, sir, I have been assured there is no doubt in the matter.'

'Bloody good riddance,' said Marriott.

'Whilst I am still here, you will kindly refrain from such unnecessary comment,' was Traynton's inevitable reply.

'Have the police made any progress?' asked Spender.

'I think not, sir, despite the attendance of a host of men. I know of nothing.'

'If you don't, nobody will.'

Traynton looked pleased at such a compliment.

Spender left the clerks' room. Curious about the details

of the murder, he went into Holter's room. The only obvious signs of what had happened were the carpetless floor, the damaged bookcase, and the rough outline of a body in white tape near the desk.

He stared at the tape. There lay Corry, so to speak, and that was an incredible fact.

'Good morning, sir,' said a deep voice from behind him. Startled, he turned to see two men had come into the room.

'You must be Mr Spender?'

'Yes, I am.'

'I'm Detective Inspector Brock and this is Detective Constable Yawley. Would it be convenient to have a word or two with you?'

'Sure. You'd better come into my room.'

Once in Spender's room and sitting down, Brock spoke. 'One of my chaps saw you yesterday evening, of course, but I thought I ought to have a word with you myself. I gather you didn't know the dead man at all well?'

'He certainly wasn't a bosom pal of mine. I used to meet him here from time to time when he came to see Resse and very occasionally he'd give me a brief marked as low as possible.'

'Did you like what you knew about him?'

Brock watched the lack of expression on Spender's face and this confirmed his snap opinion that the other was a man who seldom, if ever, said all that he felt or thought.

'He wasn't a man one did like,' said Spender, after a short pause.

'So I've gathered. Everyone seems to have detested him.'

'Always with reason, no doubt.'

'Did you have a reason?'

Spender continued to speak casually. 'I? No. We've never really had much contact.'

Brock spoke equally casually. 'When was your car accident?'

'Car accident?'

'Haven't you had one recently?'

'No.'

'Are you quite certain?'

'There's no one can be more certain. Why?'

'I had an anonymous letter this morning referring me to it.'

Spender's face at last showed signs of emotion. 'What the hell? I haven't done more than scrape a wing in the last ten years.'

'May I see your driving licence?'

Spender took out his wallet and passed it across. Brock checked that there were no endorsements and returned it. 'You haven't had an accident that hasn't been reported?'

'No. Look, just because some...'

'What garage do you go to, sir?'

'The local village one. What are you going to do? Find out if I'm lying and whether they've tidied up torn wings or washed off any blood?'

'We'll be doing that, sir. We may not believe anonymous information, but we have to follow it up.'

'No matter how ridiculous it is?'

'That's right.'

'Is there supposed to be a connection between this accident that never was and the murder, then?'

'The letter was suggesting that.'

Spender leaned back in his chair. 'Something as far-fetched as a concealed car accident, Corry the only witness, and my being blackmailed by him ever since?'

'That's quite an idea.'

'And I might be telling it to you in order to make you think I must be innocent to do so?'

'You could be. A quick look through your bank balances may tell us whether you are.'

Spender took a packet of cigarettes from his pocket and offered it. Brock accepted a cigarette, but Yawley refused with a gesture of repugnance.

'There's always a lot of dirty washing brought to light in a case like this, isn't there?' said Spender.

'Quite often, yes, sir, but not merely because someone likes producing it.'

'I wasn't suggesting it was one of your pleasures.' Spender drew on his cigarette. The smoke was caught by the breeze from the opened window and was quickly dispersed. 'Corry never used anything but dirty linen.'

Brock crossed his legs. 'You told my chap that you didn't get home Tuesday night until after seven?'

'Does that leave me without an alibi?'

Brock ignored the question. 'You said you had a puncture on the way home which was what delayed you so much. I suppose you took the tyre to a garage?'

'Yes.'

'And they mended it?'

For the first time, Spender's voice expressed his growing uneasiness. 'They checked everything, but said there wasn't a puncture. The valve must have temporarily gone on the blink.'

'Only temporarily?'

'They couldn't really find anything wrong with it, but they replaced it.'

'And the tyre?'

'Has been all right ever since. I suppose that all sounds like... like so much nonsense?'

'I shouldn't worry, sir, I've heard much worse,' replied Brock enigmatically. He stood up, thanked Spender, and left the room. Yawley followed him outside and closed the door. 'Get on to the lab,' said Brock, 'and find out if they've analysed that powder yet? Tell 'em they've had enough time to make the stuff. In the meantime, I'm going into the clerks' room.'

'Yes, sir.'

Brock entered the clerks' room. Only Marriott was there and he was typing. Brock, wondering if he were committing sacrilege, sat down in Traynton's chair.

Marriott stopped typing and leaned back. 'How's the case going?' he asked.

'As they all go. In fits and starts, two steps forwards and one backwards.'

'It must have been someone from outside.'

'Must it?'

Marriott spoke quickly. 'I was talking to a solicitor's clerk and he says that Corry had a lot of shady clients for whom he did the kind of work he shouldn't have done. One of 'em must have come and shot him.'

'It's possible,' agreed Brock. 'But can you suggest why this shady client should have bothered to come all the way to chambers, how he got in, and how Corry got in?'

'It's only a suggestion. I thought you'd want to know.'

'Thanks.'

Marriott hesitated and then resumed his typing. He completed one line and was half-way through the next one when he swore as he pressed the wrong key.

'I must be putting you off,' said Brock. 'Tell you what, just help me for a few minutes and then I'll leave you alone. Give me a check on the time you left chambers last night.'

'I've already said half a dozen times. I caught my usual bus and walked straight back from the stop and if my parents hadn't been out, they'd have told you just that.'

'I was asking you about last night, not Tuesday night,' said Brock patiently.

'Last night?'

'That's it.'

'But why?'

'That doesn't matter just now. Did you leave here early?'

'Me? With Old Misery around?'

'Who was here when you finally left?'

'Well, there was Mr Resse and ... I don't think there was anyone else.'

'One more thing – how many typewriters are there around?'

'Typewriters? The two in here and that's all. Except for the portable that Mr Spender brings in sometimes.'

As Brock stood up, he sighed. 'God, it's hot! Have you two pieces of typing paper I can have?'

Marriott passed two sheets of paper over and watched as the detective inserted one of these in the free typewriter and typed rapidly. Then, at a polite request, he pulled out of the typewriter he had been using the draft statement of claim and stood to one side.

Brock typed out a couple of lines with the second typewriter. He unwound the paper. 'Thanks very much. Sorry to have disturbed your work.'

'What's it all in aid of?'

'A simple little test.'

'You all seem to be doing a hell of a lot of little tests.'

'Now you know something about the work that goes into a case before it reaches court ... and some clever counsel does his damndest to rip it to shreds,' replied Brock, showing considerable feeling.

Brock left chambers five minutes later. He spoke to the sole waiting reporter and promised a news conference at six o'clock that evening, then went down to the street and climbed into his car which he had parked in front of the building, close to a no-parking sign.

On arrival at the police station, he went into the general room and told the duty sergeant to get someone to take the samples of typewriting to Maidstone for expert comparison tests at HQ. The duty sergeant said no men were available, but the DI merely dropped a large envelope on to the counter. After that, he walked to his room and as soon as he was inside he stripped off his coat, loosened his tie, and sat down.

The telephone rang. The detective superintendent wanted to know how things were going. Brock said it had been confirmed that the locks of the two outside doors of chambers had not been forced, that of the suspects only Aiden and Joan Fleming had worthwhile alibis, that everybody in the world hated Corry, that an anonymous letter had been received, and that no further information had come in from the laboratories. The detective superintendent said it sounded as if little or no progress had been made. On that sour note, the telephone conversation ended.

Reluctantly, Brock decided he must attempt to catch up with some of the routine work and he was in the middle of reading a report on a minor breaking and entering when the telephone rang again. He cursed as he picked up the receiver.

'Inspector Brock,' said the civilian telephonist who manned the switchboard during the day, 'there's a call I think you ought to deal with.'

'Isn't there anyone else around?' he answered wearily.

'It's to do with the Corry case.'

'All right.' He lit a cigarette as he waited. The telephone clicked twice and a man said: 'Hullo?'

'Detective Inspector Brock speaking.'

'My name's Ted Wallace. Look, I've been reading about the murder and there's something you ought to hear about. My wife says it doesn't mean nothing and I'm stupid to go on about it, but as I told her, she don't know what's important and what ain't. Only the police know that.'

'That's quite right.' The caller's eager, self-assertive voice caused the DI, admittedly solely from bias, to imagine him to be small, belligerent, and as untrustworthy as a car salesman.

'Well, it was like this. The bloke was killed on Tuesday, wasn't he?'

'That's right.'

'In that building in the High Street what's between the optician's and the post office? Looks like a private house with a bit of garden?'

'Yes.'

'I was going past there just before a quarter to seven.' The caller waited as if this statement should have occasioned great surprise. After a while, he continued in disappointed tones. 'I know what the time was because the church clock struck just afterwards and that ain't never wrong, is it?'

'I doubt it.'

'I saw a woman coming out of that house. Almost running, she was, looking like she was really terrified.'

Brock discounted the description of her expression because most people had a too imaginative memory in a case like this, but there must have been some reason for the man's noticing her. 'What first made you look at her?'

There was a salacious chuckle. 'She was wearing one of them dresses.'

'Topless?' Even as he put the question, Brock thought how remote was the possibility of such a thing in a town of the stifling respectability of Hertonhurst.

'No such luck. But it dipped down in the front as if it weren't never going to stop. Made me think they was going to come popping out. But they didn't.'

'Can you describe the woman?'

'I didn't properly see her face on account of watching her dress,' said Wallace, forgetting his earlier description of her look of terror. 'She was come and gone so quickly.'

'I can understand where your attention lay.' Brock managed to sound heartily man-to-man.

There was a snigger.

'Any idea what colour her hair was?' asked Brock.

'She was a blonde.'

'Was she wearing a lot of make-up?'

'Well, I ... I think so.'

Brock quickly made up his mind. 'All right, Mr Wallace, let's rest it there for a moment. You have a really good think and I'll send an officer along to have a chat with you and get as good a description as you can give him. Would you like to see him at work or at your house?'

'Don't matter. I'm at the bakers in Satchell Street and my house is in Finsbury Terrace: number twelve. It's painted red.'

'Thanks.' Brock wrote the information down on the pad in front of him. 'By the way, any idea what colour the dress was?'

'Pink. With her blonde hair it made me think of strawberries and cream.'

After replacing the receiver, Brock stared down at the writing pad. If Wallace could not be more precise, his evidence would be useful but not conclusive. Brock wondered how best to obtain a photograph of Charlotte Holter for Wallace to see and he decided that the offices of *Kent Life* would probably be able to help: she was the type of woman who would frequently be photographed.

The case was beginning to show form and logic.

* * *

Holter, after appearing at Ashford County Court for an elderly and pugnacious woman who did not mind how much she spent on a case she had brought 'For the principle of the thing,' drove back to Crighton and arrived home at 1.10 PM.

As he stepped on to the drive, Charlotte came running out of the house. 'What's happened?' she asked breathlessly.

He looked at her in some astonishment. 'How d'you mean, Betty?'

'Why have you come back here in the middle of the day? Something must have happened?'

'But you asked me to come back to lunch if I possibly could. The case came to a quick end when the other side collapsed.'

'Oh!' She fidgeted with the front of her dress. 'Of course I did. I'm being very silly.'

'What on earth did you think had happened?'

'Just for the moment, I thought you must be in some terrible trouble.'

'Me?' he laughed. 'Show me the trouble I can't get out of!' He put his arm round her waist. 'The other Silks on the circuit would like to see me drop down dead so they can have my work, but they aren't going to have that pleasure for a long, long time yet. Being married to you means I'm as frisky as a twenty-year-old. I told old Jim, when he complained he was feeling old and decrepit, that if he'd married someone young and beautiful he wouldn't have two toes in the grave now.'

'Radwick, what have the police been doing in chambers?'

He ignored her question. 'Last night was wonderful, wasn't it? I wasn't tired, you see. If we get to bed early tonight ...'

Her voice was shrill as she put the question for the second time: 'What have the police been doing in chambers?' She stepped clear of his grasp.

He answered in an aggrieved tone of voice. 'You know I haven't been in chambers this morning, Betty. I expect they're snooping around somewhere, asking a lot of damn-fool questions. What's it matter what they're doing?'

She had been about to say something, but she checked herself. She stepped close to him and replaced his arm around herself. 'Of course it doesn't matter, darling. And you're quite right, last night was wonderful.'

He smiled complacently as they walked into the house.

Except when they had guests, they often ate lunch in the breakfast-room since it was nearer the kitchen than the dining-room. Agnes Utley brought in two chops and Charlotte served them both to her husband. He asked her why she was eating only salad and she replied she was going to diet to try to lose a few pounds around her waist.

He was half-way through his meal when she spoke once more, obliquely at first, about the question of what action the police were taking. 'Radwick, how's Oliver?'

He swallowed a mouthful before answering. 'Never

changes, poor devil. Still playing around with briefs marked in single figures.'

'Have the police questioned him?'

'They've been worrying the lives of all of us.' He helped himself to another potato and a large pat of butter.

'Does it upset him at all?'

'You can never tell with Oliver. He's damned odd in many ways. Reminds me of Cassius, lean and hungry.'

'D'you think they've any idea yet about what really happened?'

'Who?'

'The police,' she said sharply. She hastily spoke far more softly. 'It's all so interesting for me, Radwick.' She reached across the small circular table and rested her hand on his as he was about to raise the laden fork to his mouth. 'You don't really mind me asking you, do you?'

He looked at her. She hadn't changed a bit in the four years of their marriage. Her blonde hair was as perfectly blonde, her face was still smooth enough for a girl of sixteen, and as on the day of their marriage her mouth invited and her body promised.

'What are you thinking?' she asked.

'Only how extremely attractive you are,' he replied, with overdone gallantry.

'You looked angry.'

'Well, I wasn't, because I was remembering last night.'

'Can't you ever talk of anything else? Isn't there anything else in the world?'

'What's wrong with talking about it?' he asked, surprised.

She fidgeted with the fork on her plate. 'Nothing, but it seems odd in the middle of a meal.'

'Isn't it more fun to be odd?'

'I ... I suppose so. I'm sorry I'm snappy, darling, but I haven't been feeling completely well.'

He was immediately worried. 'What's wrong? Have you called in the doctor?'

'There's no need for that, it's only the heat, or something.'

'You poor darling.'

'Oh, Radwick, you're so wonderful and understanding! I wish I could show you just how much I love you.'

He finished eating his chop. He was pleased with himself, but then a man had a right to be when his wife was as beautiful as Charlotte was and she confessed that she loved him more than she could show.

Chapter Nine

BROCK WAS A MAN who hated criminals. He hated them whether they had been guilty of a mean theft or a brutal murder because they were the people who could destroy any democracy, by which he meant the right of every person, within obvious limits, to live the kind of life he wanted to. Brock hated the murderer of Corry, even though it was obvious that the solicitor had a warped and very unpleasant character, and it was because of this that he doggedly continued to work with scant regard to the hours. He drove up to Rachael West's house at 7.35 in the evening.

The two hundred-year-old house, orginally of clapboard, had been cleverly modernized in a way that allowed moddernisations to live in harmony with the ancient structure. As Brock climbed out of his car, he looked through the nearer window and saw a woman, sitting in a chair. He crossed to front door and rang the bell.

The door was opened by the woman he had just seen. She stood a foot shorter than he and was dressed in a cotton shirt and a pair of grey flannel trousers. Her hair was cut short and straight and she wore neither make-up nor jewellery. 'I'm Detective Inspector Brock, county constabulary. Miss West?'

'Yes.'

'I'd like to have a word with you if it's convenient?'

She studied him for a few seconds and then pushed the

door more fully open. 'You'd better come in. What's the matter?' Her voice was harsh and she spoke abruptly, as if in a perpetual hurry.

They went into the room on the right, the one which he had seen when he arrived.

'Take a seat,' she said.

He sat down, carefully, on a chair of modern design which looked as if it might either collapse or turn over under his weight. It did neither and after a while he relaxed.

'What d'you want?' she asked, as she sat down.

'It's the Corry case, Miss West.'

'Well?' She picked up a packet of cigarettes from the glass-topped table immediately in front of her. 'D'you smoke?'

'Yes, I do.'

She helped herself to a cigarette and then tossed the packet over to him.

'I think you know Mrs Holter?' he said, after striking a match which gave both of them a light.

'I design some of her clothes and have them made up.'

'As routine, we naturally have to check up where people were at certain times. Mrs Holter says she was here on Tuesday evening. Can you confirm that?'

'Yes, I can.'

'All the evening?'

'She arrived some time after five and didn't leave until after eight.'

'I suppose you were working on something for her?'

'Yes.'

'Does she visit you often?'

'I can't see that that's of any interest to you.'

'Why not, Miss West?'

'Because it has nothing to do with the death of this man.'

He appeared to be placidly unaffected by her openly expressed antagonism. 'It's almost impossible at the moment to say what is connected with Corry's death and what isn't.'

'Then find out the answers to that before you start asking people questions.'

He smiled. 'I'm afraid I've become hardened to my own impertinence.' He looked round for an ash-tray.

'On your right.'

He stroked the ash from his cigarette into a small china hollow-backed dog which, until she had spoken, he had thought to be a hideous *objet d'art*. 'How often has Mrs Holter visited you in the past month, Miss West?'

'I've no idea.'

'You wouldn't like to hazard a guess?'

'I should not.'

'I see.'

'What do you see?'

He smiled again. 'I hope I'm not interrupting any work?'

'That depends on how much longer you're staying?'

'You do work in the evenings, then?'

'I've already told you that that's when Mrs Holter came here.'

'You won't mind signing a statement, will you, Miss West?'

'What d'you mean?' she asked sharply.

'It'll only be to say that Mrs Holter was here last Tuesday evening from some time after five o'clock to just after eight.'

'Why should I have to sign anything?'

'It's a formality. If there's a trial I'm afraid you'll be called as a witness.'

She stubbed out the cigarette she had been smoking and lit another. Her fingers, long and elegant and in sharp contrast with the rest of her body, were badly stained a nicotine yellow. 'If I've got to sign, I've got to.'

His voice remained quiet and easy. 'And will your evidence under oath be the same as you've just given me?'

'How dare you suggest it won't be? I'm not a liar.'

'I hope not, Miss West, for your sake.'

'Get out of my house,' she snapped.

'Of course. But before I go, perhaps I ought to tell you that I've spoken to a man who saw a woman leave the murder building at a quarter to seven. His description of her identifies her as Mrs Holter. She wasn't really here at a quarter to seven, was she?'

Rachael West drew twice on her cigarette, then stubbed it out with such force that the paper split and tobacco spilled out. She looked at the detective, stood up and walked across to the small built-in cupboard on the far wall. She took out a bottle of whisky and a glass and poured herself out a large whisky which she drank neat. 'Why didn't you have the decency to tell me that at the beginning?'

'In my job, we have to try to understand people, to be able to evaluate them.'

'All right, so now you think you understand me. Get out and leave me alone.'

'When did she leave? Or wasn't she ever here?'

'I don't know what the time was. I'm not some bloody time-keeper.'

'It takes roughly half an hour to drive from here to the High Street in Hertonhurst. My guess is she left here around a quarter to six?'

'I've said I've no idea.'

'Did she borrow your car?'

'Yes.'

'How often did she do this sort of thing?'

'I never counted.'

'But this wasn't the first time?'

'No.'

'What dress was she wearing on Tuesday?'

'I can't remember.'

'That can't be true, Miss West. As a designer, you're surely bound to have noticed, especially as you may even have designed it yourself?'

'Do you have to be so bloody polite about it all?' she said loudly.

'I can very easily be ruder if you prefer.'

'It was the Milano line. Knee length, high waist, no belt, slashed V neck, narrow collar, three-quarter sleeves, and two pleats at the back giving a full back and tight front. The buttons are large and covered with the material of the dress.'

'And what was the colour?'

'Tide-side pink.'

'What's that like?'

'A bright strawberry pink.'

'Thank you very much, Miss West.'

She muttered something and turned her back on him as

she poured herself another drink. He left and returned to his car. As he started the engine he momentarily wondered what had secured Rachael West's loyalty to Charlotte Holter when on the face of it she could have been expected to hate the younger and far more attractive woman.

He drove to Hertonhurst along the back route and when he reached the crest of the hills he stopped the car in the lay-by. The view was one he often sought out. Below was the land, seen as if from an aircraft, a series of small patches in an infinite variety of greens and browns. Beyond was the English Channel and the French coast, a low-lying smudge of grey.

He thought about the case. Charlotte Holter had been in chambers on Tuesday evening. That was certain, even if it could not yet be proved. She had been in the room when Corry was shot. He visualized her sharp, smart beauty and tried to gauge how panicky she probably was by now.

After twenty minutes, he regretfully started the engine, backed out on to the road, and continued on to Hertonhurst and Oliver Resse's house.

Resse lived in a part of the town which was gradually decaying, but which had not yet decayed. Most of the people there were in the same position he was: professional class by upbringing and instinct, but not by income. The badly designed Victorian houses were almost all in need of considerable repair.

Brock parked his car and walked up the small front garden in which the two beds were filled with weeds and the grass needed cutting. He climbed the half-dozen stone steps and knocked on the front door. It was opened by a woman, Mrs Resse, to whom he introduced himself. She showed him into the sitting-room, the furniture of which was almost as well worn as in his own police house.

Very shortly afterwards, Resse came into the room, wearing an open-necked shirt and a pair of worn and creased grey flannel trousers. He shook hands. 'This is unexpected, Inspector, but I hesitate at this early stage to add that it's also a pleasure.'

'Very wise of you, sir.'

Resse laughed, a trifle too loudly, as he indicated the

arm-chairs. 'Have a pew and a drink? I can offer you Empire sherry or a beer?'

'I'll take a beer off you and I admit that it'll be a pleasure.'

'You do know, don't you, that you can't drink with a man and then arrest him? It's considered frightfully unsporting, like shooting a sitting duck.'

'This isn't a very sporting case.'

Showing the sense of uncertainty he felt, Resse hesitated, then turned and left the room. He returned with two pewter mugs filled with beer. After handing the detective one mug, he raised his own. 'To a long friendship and may it never end.'

Brock lifted his own mug. 'The first today and doubly welcome for that.'

'But I thought detectives spent their lives surrounded by brandies and broads?'

'Unfortunately, not in Kent, sir. No saying what goes on in other counties, of course.' Brock put his mug down on a small wooden coffee table and began to search his pockets. At first, Resse tried to appear uninterested, but after a while he stared directly at the detective. He began to fidget his arms.

Brock eventually brought out three sheets of paper which he unfolded and smoothed down over his knee. 'I was sent an anonymous letter this morning,' he said.

'Good God!' exclaimed Resse. He realized he had spoken too theatrically and hastily added: 'But I suppose that happens quite often?' He sat down in the second armchair and a spring twanged.

'I wouldn't say that. The last one was almost a month ago. A woman complained that her neighbour was a sex maniac. She spent six months in a mental hospital but they say she's cured now.'

'Really?'

Brock examined each of the sheets in turn. He looked up and spoke in his usual amiable voice. 'You wrote the letter, of course?'

'No,' said Resse loudly. 'Why the hell should I do a thing like that?'

'To try to divert suspicion away from yourself.'

'Look, I'm not a fool and I wouldn't..."
'You're not a fool by a heck of a long way, Mr Resse, but you don't seem to know much about the abilities of the average detective. I typed out the same message on the two typewriters in chambers and sent all the typing off for examination. Traynton's machine was the one used by the anonymous writer. The paper is identical with the paper in chambers.'

'If it was Traynton's machine, he probably wrote the message.'

'You were the last person to leave chambers yesterday evening.'

'I ... I may have been. I just don't know.'

'It's an important point.'

'Why?'

'The person who typed this letter would have wanted to be on his own when he did it.'

'It wasn't I. D'you think I'm the kind of man to write anonymous letters?'

'Normally, not in a thousand years.'

'Then why name me now?'

'You forgot to include yourself in the list of the accused: if someone else had been the writer, your name would have been there. Another point, things aren't normal for you: you had a row with a man not long before he was murdered. That means you're panicky and concerned with only one thing – trying to prove you weren't the murderer. Panic changes a man's character pretty damn' quickly.'

Resse's face flushed and as he drank, his hand trembled. He put the mug down on the coffee table. 'I said to you it had become a case of *sauve qui peut*.'

'Yes, you did.'

'I sent the bloody thing and that made me feel like some dirty little back street Arab. Holter's always talking about the brotherhood of the Bar, but as far as I'm concerned there's precious little relationship left. I had a row with Corry on Tuesday, a really good, bitter, vocal row. I became so angry I was brave enough to tell him what I thought of him, a man who'd not pay his debts just for the pleasure of seeing someone squirm. He jeered at me. He asked me whether all my expensive education had done me two-pence worth of good and whether my wife's great and noble relations helped to support me. I was going to hit him.'

'Did you?'

Resse ran the back of his hand across his forehead, as if vainly trying to erase the memory. 'He stood there and went on taunting me. He said that if I did hit him, he'd not only not pay me a penny of all he owed me, he'd also never send me another brief.' Resse, his expression one of pain, looked at the detective. 'You're making me strip myself.'

'It can sometimes be a good thing.'

'And very amusing for others?'

'I've learned never to laugh at other people's misfortunes, Mr Resse. It's a trite thing to say, but the man who slips on a banana skin usually hurts himself.'

Resse stared at the far wall. 'A question I had often asked myself – I'm indecently introspective – was whether I'd find the courage to tell him to go to hell if ever it reached that point. Can a man really sell his self-respect for a mere five hundred pounds a year? That row gave me the answer. I didn't hit Corry. "Ful wys is he that can him-selven knowe." But who wants that sort of corroding wisdom?' Resse finished the beer in his mug. 'But you're not interested in the sordid confessions of a middle-aged failure. All you want to know is whether I shot Corry because of the row we had.'

'Did you?'

'No. Is it any good, in support of my denial, pointing out that having grovelled before his threats of cutting off a large proportion of my income, I'd hardly be likely to kill him later and so lose everything once and for all?'

'I haven't forgotten that fact.'

Regaining some of his normal ironic pugnacity, Resse said: 'I feel justified in keeping it constantly before you.' He looked at his empty mug and stood up. 'Have another beer?'

Brock hesitated.

'It's all right, Inspector. No matter how embittered I feel, I can't in honesty claim that two more bottles of beer will exhaust my cellar.'

'Thanks very much, sir. I'd like another.'

Resse left the room and soon came back with two half-pint bottles of beer which he opened.

After he had filled his mug, Brock raised it quickly and drank. 'Nothing could be more welcome. When I retire I think I'll keep a pub and grow really fat.' He put the mug down on the table once more. 'Mr Spender denies any accident in his car.'

'It was the best I could think up. Corry might have been blackmailing him for an accident he hadn't reported. It was the kind of thing Corry would have enjoyed doing.'

'And your accusation against Mrs Holter?'

'I made that up as well. I can't claim to a very original brain.'

'You didn't really make that bit up, did you?'

Resse drank. 'I just wrote the first thing that occurred to me.'

'I already knew she was having an affair.'

Resse turned slightly until he could look straight at the detective. 'D'you swear that's the truth?'

'Yes.'

'Thanks for helping me to salve the remnant of my conscience.'

'Have you forgotten it's a case of murder? Is your conscience more important?'

'To me, yes.' Resse offered a packet of cigarettes. 'A couple of months ago I was walking along the High Street fairly late on in the evening, somewhere about nine. When I was level with chambers, Charlotte Holter came out of the building. She saw me as she reached the pavement and she looked as though the last trump had just been blown in her ear. She recovered her natural – poise, I have heard it called – and told me she'd lost one of her small gold charms from her bracelet and had been looking in chambers to see whether it was there. Her husband had gone over to Canterbury to give one of his after-dinner talks, so she'd borrowed his keys and gone into chambers to look for the charm which had great sentimental value. I politely asked her if she'd found it and then even more politely raised my hat, wished her good evening, and went on my way. I'd forgotten the incident when, by pure chance, I was in the clerks' room next morning as Holter asked Josephus Traynton for his keys which he'd given to Traynton the previous morning so that they could be taken to an ironmongers to have a couple of spare sets cut.'

'Is that all?' asked Brock.

'Anti-climax? Obviously, she could have been in chambers for some very ordinary reason and when she came face to face with me she was so startled she said the first thing that came to mind?'

'I don't believe that because, as I've already said, I know she was having an affair.'

Resse spoke bitterly. 'What should any man expect when he marries a tart of half his age?'

'The really odd thing is that each and every one of them honestly expects a faithful wife.'

Chapter Ten

THE COLOURS in the Holters' bedroom were as striking as anywhere in the house. On three walls the wall-paper was deep blue background with light blue and gold designs and on the fourth wall and ceiling was a rich crimson paper. The off-set pillar which supported part of the ceiling (originally this had been two rooms) was covered with gold leaf. The headboards were gold painted and the bed covers were light blue. The floor was dark and light green in alternating triangles.

Holter went into the small dressing-room and changed into his pyjamas, glad to be out of sight since his portly figure could, in cold blood, look rather ridiculous. When he returned to the bedroom, Charlotte had just put on her nightdress. It was semi-transparent.

He crossed to her side, but when he tried to kiss her she turned her head away.

'I'd rather we didn't tonight, Radwick,' she said.

'But I'm not in the least bit tired.'

'Why can't you ever leave me alone? You're always after me.'

Her strained expression made her look almost ugly.

'I am your husband,' he said pompously.

'You're a randy old goat.'

He stepped away from her. 'I am not all that old.'

She forced herself to act more calmly. 'Radwick, my darling, I didn't mean that kind of old. You must know I wouldn't mean it like that.'

'I've always hoped you wouldn't.' He was silent for a few seconds, then said: 'Why can't we play ding-a-ling?'

'I don't feel like it.'

'What's wrong? Isn't a husband supposed to feel randy?'

'Of course he is.'

'Then why did you say what you did?'

'Darling, it was just because I was feeling worn out. Don't you see that I was really complimenting you? I wouldn't have married you unless I'd known you'd want to play ding-a-ling all day and all night long.'

Slowly, she climbed into bed. As she sat upright, leaning against the headboard, the light showed the outline of her breasts.

His mind was filled with uncertainty. Was her refusal an adamant one? Sometimes, her mood changed abruptly and where before she had refused, she now welcomed. He remembered one such occasion, but then a further memory worried him: wasn't that one of the times when he had been too tired? He couldn't be certain because he did everything possible to erase such memories. He studied her and regretfully became certain she had not changed her mind. He walked round to the far side of the bed and climbed in.

'Don't be too angry with me, Radwick,' she said, in a wheedling voice.

'I'm not at all,' he answered coldly.

'You are. Just a teeny little bit.'

He remained silent.

'You know how much I love, love, love you.'

'Do you?'

'Honestly, that's not a serious question, is it? Darling, I adore you so much it hurts.' She leaned across and kissed him, but the moment he raised his right hand she returned to her half of the bed.

He picked up the book from the bed-side table. He was sorry they weren't going to, but at least he was freed from the worry of whether it would work, or not. He began to read.

'Radwick.'

'Yes?' He was irritated. Once he had begun to read, he disliked being interrupted.

'I . . . I don't like what's happening.'

He put his book down on the bed, carefully holding it so that he did not lose the place. 'What on earth are you talking about, darling?'

'You know I went and saw Rachael this evening, after she'd telephoned me?'

'Yes. Why you keep on seeing her I . . .'

'The police have been along to her.'

'Have they?'

'They asked her where I was on Tuesday evening. Radwick, I'm frightened.'

'Why on earth?'

'It's just that they frighten me.'

'There's absolutely no need to be, but I'll tell them to stop it immediately. They'll learn I'm not Joe Bloggs from the council house who doesn't know his rights.'

'Rachael says the detective kept on and on at her until . . . until she had to . . .' She looked quickly at him.

'Had to what?'

'Well. Tell him that as a matter of fact I wasn't with her all Tuesday evening.' She began to finger the sheet.

He spoke angrily. 'It's none of their business where you were. They've no right to go round annoying you. I'll ring the chief constable and complain.'

She noticed she was kneading the sheet and stopped, but almost immediately she began to do so again. 'I told you, didn't I, darling, that I left Rachael's just before six o'clock?'

'Did you? I don't know that I remember.'

'The detective bullied and bullied Rachael until she told him this.'

'I can promise you he won't bully anyone again.'

'You see, Radwick, I was so worried about us that I went for a drive round the countryside.'

'What were you worried about?'

'You'd been cross with me and I was terribly afraid you were beginning not to love me any more.'

His voice expressed his amazement. 'You silly little girl. As if I could ever stop loving you! How could you begin to think such a thing?'

She momentarily touched his hand. 'You're so wonderful to me.'

'Because I want to be.'

'Radwick, the detective told Rachael I was seen leaving your chambers on Tuesday evening at a quarter to seven. I swear I wasn't anywhere near there. I swear it.'

'Of course you weren't.'

'You do believe me, don't you? I promise you, I wasn't anywhere near there at the time.'

'The man's mad.'

'But I'm frightened.'

'There's absolutely no need to be frightened.'

'He must think I had something to do with the murder. But I wasn't there. I swear I wasn't there.'

He spoke furiously. 'I'll teach him that he can't slander people and get away with it.'

'You don't really believe I was anywhere near chambers, do you?'

'Of course I don't.'

'Oh, my darling, I've been so worried in case you did. You're so wonderful. It's no wonder I love you a thousand times more than anybody else in the world.'

She leaned across the bed and kissed him again, but when he raised his hand this time she did not move. After a while they played ding-a-ling: quite successfully.

* * *

Early Friday morning, Brock was given a report from the chemist who had analysed the powder which had come from the carpet in the murder room: it was face powder and reference to records and to the firm concerned showed that it was manufactured by Juliette Drage, Ltd. The powder was known as Drage 325.

DC Yawley was ordered to make inquiries at the various chemists in Hertonhurst. The first one he visited was the large one at the north end of the High Street where he spoke to a highly made-up female assistant who examined his shabby appearance with obvious distaste.

Yawley explained the purpose of his visit and, reluctantly, the assistant went away to speak to the manager. She returned and showed the detective into the office beyond the dispensing area. The manager was a small, fussy man, obsessed with a sense of his own importance.

'Drage's goods?' said the manager. 'Yes, we stock some of their lines, even though this isn't the town for their products.'

'Why's that?'

'How much d'you know about the cosmetics trade?'

'Nothing,' replied Yawley.

'Drage's stuff is probably the most expensive on the market. Most of it's imported. Their prices are twice the normal range and that's all right in London or the Midlands where the women have more money than sense, but down here in Hertonhurst there just isn't enough money available for such things.'

'D'you sell much of their face powder called three two five?'

The manager shrugged his shoulders. 'I doubt it.'

'Could you check your records?'

'Probably.'

'And give me the names of the people who buy it?'

'Only if the assistant can remember. The records won't show that.'

'If you can find out what you can.'

The manager heaved an obvious sigh. 'I'm a very busy man, but I'll do what's possible. But you'll please understand that all these interruptions make life very difficult for me.'

The manager looked through some books and then, muttering to himself, went out of the office and through the dispensing area. He returned within three minutes. 'We sell very little of that powder: so little we only hold it against definite orders.'

'Have you found out any names?'

'One of my assistants says that Mrs Rennett always has it. She's a very rich woman, of course.'

'No one else?'

'Hang on, hang on. I'm just coming to that. Another woman is Mrs Holter. She's young and very attractive, wife of that lawyer. I don't know if you know her?'

Chapter Eleven

ON HIS ARRIVAL at chambers, Holter went into the clerks' room and found only Marriott was present. 'Where's Josephus?'

'He's just telephoned, sir, to say he's caught a very heavy cold and so won't be in today.'

'Hell! I'm in court after lunch and I particularly wanted him with me.'

'I've arranged for Mrs Fleming to come here all the afternoon, sir, so that I shall be able to go with you to Maidstone.'

Holter went over to the mirror and studied his reflection. He fiddled with his tie. 'What's the use of that? If a solicitor telephones her about a brief she'll make a hopeless mess of things.'

'No, sir,' said Marriott eagerly. 'I've told her to ask the solicitor to ring again tomorrow when I'll be around to deal with things.'

Holter was almost annoyed that everything had been arranged: he was in a temper and looking for a means of venting some of it. He turned away from the mirror. 'Get on to the police, George, and speak to whoever's in charge and say that I want to see the detective inspector here, in these chambers, as soon as possible.'

'Yes, sir.' Marriott hesitated, then asked: 'Has something happened?'

'I intend to teach him a very sharp lesson. He may be used to riding high-handed over the ordinary people, George, and that's probably the best way of handling 'em, but he's going to learn he's a fool to try that sort of thing with me.'

'What's been going on, sir?'

'His men have been upsetting a friend of my wife's by making the wildest accusations.'

'What kind of accusations?'

'Never mind that now. Just give my message to them. Is there anything fresh in today?'

'Yes, sir,' Marriott picked up a brief. 'You're being asked for, special, on the Midland circuit.'

'Am I indeed?' Holter took the brief. 'That's not bad going, eh, George? They've got some reasonably good men up there, but they come all the way down here for me! And at a ripe old figure.' Holter dropped the brief on to Marriott's desk. 'Who fixed the fee that high?'

'I did, Mr Holter.'

'Did you, by God! Then there's going to be no holding you when old Josephus leaves us, eh?'

Resse hurried into the room. When he saw Holter was there he momentarily stopped, but he finally stepped over to the mantelpiece and nodded. ''Morning, Radwick. It seems that people are turning up earlier and earlier. I wonder if that makes worms of us who don't.'

'What's that?' demanded Holter.

'A random and undoubtedly stray thought.' Resse turned to Marriott. 'Well, George, what's in the post for me?'

'Nothing this morning, sir,' said Marriott, and his tone of voice suggested that this was not to be wondered at.

'Unfortunately, counsel's job is one in which it certainly isn't a case of no news being good news. No news is no briefs.'

'I've been briefed special in the Midlands,' said Holter.

'Have you indeed?'

'At a damned good figure, I don't mind admitting.'

'No, I don't suppose you do.'

Holter ignored Resse, who always seemed to begrudge the success of others, and spoke to Marriott. 'George, get on to the police now.'

'Anything wrong?' asked Resse, too casually.

'I'm going to put a stop once and for all to that detective's impertinence.'

'Has he been worrying you?'

'He's poking and prying into Charlotte's life and upsetting her and I'm not the man to stand for that.'

'No. No, of course not.'

'It's just bloody impertinence.' Holter waited for any comment, but when there was none he left and went through to his room. He sat down behind the desk. The carpet was missing, the revolver was not in the cabinet, and the top of one bookcase had had a square of wood cut out of it, but otherwise everything was just as it had been. When the carpet and the revolver were returned and the bookcase was mended, there would be nothing to mark the death of Corry.

He thought about Brock's insolence for a short while, then switched his mind – with an ease which explained some of his success – to his work. He slipped off the red tape from one of the three briefs on his desk and opened it out to read the notes he had made the previous day. Five cases had to be checked to see if they helped him. He lifted the telephone receiver. 'George, I want one Weekly Law Reports fifty-nine, one Queen's Bench ninety-two ... Appeal are in here ... And two All England sixty-three.'

For an hour and a half he worked on the case. He was interrupted when the door opened and Marriott stepped just inside the room. 'Detective Inspector Brock has just arrived, sir.'

'All right. Bring him in.'

Brock came into the room. He was dressed in a light brown suit that was a bad fit and the collar of his shirt was slightly frayed.

'You've taken a long time to get here,' said Holter.

'I'm a busy man,' Brock replied equably.

Holter deliberately and rudely remained seated, fully expecting the inspector to remain standing unless he was offered a chair, but with an unchanging expression Brock moved to his right until he could sit down. He crossed his legs and waited.

'You've been annoying a friend of my wife,' snapped Holter.

'I'm sorry to hear that.'

'You've no right to do it.'

'Would you mind telling me exactly what you're referring to so that I can ...'

'You know damn' well what I'm talking about.' In court, Holter never lost his temper, but he had no such self-control when he remembered how terribly worried Charlotte had been. 'Miss West.'

'I take it she's made some sort of complaint to you?'

'Never mind what she's done. What right have you to question people about my wife's movements?'

'I'd suggest the right of any investigating officer.'

'My wife is not even remotely connected with the death of Corry.'

'I'm very sorry, but I can't agree.'

'I'm warning you, Inspector.'

'Yes, sir?'

'If you continue, I'll go straight to the chief constable.'

'Perhaps it would be best if you did that right now, sir, if that's how you feel.'

'If I do, you won't be so insolently confident. I'll tell him you've had the impertinence to suggest my wife was somewhere near these chambers last Tuesday. You can threaten some snivelling pickpocket, but you can't do it to my wife.'

'I'm afraid that when it comes to an investigation, sir, I fail to see any difference.'

'Do you, by God?'

'Yes, sir.'

'Then you'll soon find out.'

'Perhaps, Mr Holter, you'll either make an official objection about my conduct of the case or else you'll leave me to carry on as I want?'

Holter checked any further heated words. Brock must know that a man in Holter's position could make considerable trouble, given the opportunity. Brock's confidence, therefore, must stem from certainty. He firmly believed that Charlotte had been near chambers Tuesday evening. In which case he, Holter, must find out why and correct this ridiculous mistake and that could only be done by the use of tact, no matter how angry he felt. 'Inspector,' he said, in his mildest voice, 'if my tongue has walked away with me, it's because I feel very impassioned where my wife's concerned.'

'Of course, sir.' Brock's expression became one of wary watchfulness.

'I'm sure you'd feel just the same about your wife. If someone insulted her you'd very soon take up cudgels on her behalf.'

'I expect I would, yes.'

'Then you can understand that when Charlotte told me last night she was worried absolutely sick, I naturally became very angry. Not because of what you'd been doing or saying, but because of the effect that that had had on her. I'm sure you can feel sympathy for me there?'

'I can understand it, yes.'

'Good. That allows us to discuss the whole thing like two rational human beings. You had a word with Miss West and discovered Charlotte did not stay with her all Tuesday evening. That's all, isn't it?'

'Yes.'

'Well now, Inspector, why should that insignificant bit of information lead you to say all you have? Why should it concern anyone where my wife was?'

'Because there was a woman present in these chambers at the time of the shooting.'

'But what makes you so certain of that?'

'I think I'd rather just leave it at that.'

'Did someone see a woman leave the building?'

Brock was silent.

'There are other offices in this building, Inspector.'

'Quite. But all of them were empty by six o'clock.'

'Empty only so far as you know.'

'That's so.'

'Still, you don't need me to teach you your job! You have your task and I have mine and we're each best suited to our own. That being so, I'll content myself by saying that it's quite impossible Charlotte was within a dozen miles of these chambers when Corry was shot. She's assured me of that, not that I ever thought otherwise for a second.

You may have my word for it that if there was a woman present, it was not my wife.'

'Thank you for telling me,' said Brock, with the greatest politeness.

There was a knock on the door and Marriott entered. 'I wondered if you'd like some coffee, sir?'

'An excellent idea, George.' Holter spoke to Brock. 'You'll have coffee, won't you?'

'I'd like some, thanks.'

After Marriott had gone, Holter said to Brock: 'How about a cigar?'

'I'd rather ...' began the detective inspector, but he stopped speaking when he saw his words were going unheeded.

'They're not at all bad cigars which were given to me by a chap I defended successfully for fraud at the Old Bailey. That, I might say, was a case and a half!' Holter searched in one of the right-hand drawers. 'Two hundred thousand pounds missing and apparently only one man could have taken it ... Where the hell are those cigars? There's a box of fifty still half full somewhere ... The whole thing became a battle between accountants.' Impatiently, Holter slammed one drawer shut and pulled out another, searched through it, and then through the bottom one which was by far the deepest. He pulled out papers and files and stacked them on top of the desk. 'My strongest card, frankly, was his bank balances. There wasn't a penny in them there shouldn't have been and if he did pinch the money he damn' well knew how to hide it. Eh?'

'Presumably, yes.'

'Your sympathies, naturally, are all with ...' Holter stopped speaking as he began to lift out a file and there slid from inside it the heavy silver-framed photograph of Charlotte that normally stood on his desk. He wondered how he had never missed it, but clearly the heat of events had made him less observant than usual. How had it come to be in the drawer? He saw that one side of the frame was covered with a dull, brownish substance which he was certain was dried blood. The photograph must have been handled at the time of the murder. Immediately, his mind recalled the trail of blood which had led from the point where Corry had been shot to the point where the body was found, by the desk, and for the first time the reason for dragging the body across the floor became frighteningly clear to him.

'Is anything wrong?' asked Brock.

Holter, desperately trying to overcome his sense of shock, dropped the file he was holding on to the photograph. He began to pack back the papers and files which were on top of the desk. 'I just can't think where the cigars have got to.'

'Please don't worry on my account, Mr Holter. I much prefer a cigarette.'

'I suppose the police searched this desk?'

'Just a quick look in each drawer, but nothing more. We never go through personal effects unless we know there's a need to. I can assure you that no policeman has walked off with your cigars.'

Holter hastened to erase the suggestion that he had inadvertently made. 'No, of course not. I must have taken them home sometime and just completely forgotten the fact.' Marriott came into the room with a wooden tray on which were two chipped mugs filled with instant coffee, a battered jug of milk, and sugar.

Holter helped himself to sugar. 'George,' he said, 'd'you remember that box of cigars the fraud bloke gave me and which I keep in chambers?'

'Of course, sir.'

'I can't find it anywhere.'

'Have you looked through all the drawers, sir?'

'Yes.'

Marriott put the tray down. 'You'd better let me check. As Mr Traynton says, he's sure you couldn't find a haystack on a needle.' He walked round the desk.

'It's all right,' said Holter hurriedly. 'I know they're not here.'

'If I just ...'

'No, no. I must have taken them home.'

Marriott picked up the tray and left.

As he smoked a cigarette, drank the coffee, or tried to keep an intelligent conversation going, Holter kept looking at the floor as he imagined the trail of blood on the carpet. It took all his self-control to stem a rising sense of panic.

A few minutes later, Brock leaned forward, put his

empty cup on the desk, and stood up. 'If there's nothing more, then, I'll be on my way?'

'Nothing, and thanks very much for coming along.' Holter hurriedly went round the desk and shook hands. 'I'm sure it was a good idea to meet and have a chat. It clears the air when both parties know what's going on.'

'Good-bye, Mr Holter,' said Brock, 'and thanks for the coffee.' He left the room.

Holter sat down. He stared unseeingly at the papers and law books scattered over the top of his desk. In the shock of finding Charlotte's photograph with the blood on the frame, he had connected it up with the trail of blood that had marked the path which the dead Corry had been dragged along. But wasn't it ridiculous of him to suppose there was any connection? Hadn't his mind, trained to follow logical conclusions, been shocked into complete illogicality?

Logical or illogical, one thing was absolutely certain. He had to wash the blood off the frame and then take the photograph home so that no one else should ever have the same ideas as he had just had.

Taking some brown paper from one of the small drawers, he began to wrap up the framed photograph of a smiling Charlotte. God! he thought, if any of the police started thinking as he was thinking now they might really believe she had been in chambers at the time of the murder. Why couldn't that goddamn' fool of a woman, Rachael, have kept her mouth shut? No one could have proved anything. Hadn't Charlotte spent enough money with the old bitch to get some loyalty in return?

His fingers became all thumbs as he tried to fold the ends of the brown paper flat. The thought of Charlotte falsely placed in trouble increased his panicky anger and he began to curse the murderer with monotonous obscenity.

Eventually, he secured the brown paper sufficiently well and he hurried from his room to the small cloakroom, immediately opposite the clerks' room. After locking the door, he filled the basin with hot water. Then he carefully washed the blood from the ornate silver frame, using a small scrubbing brush. When satisfied he had removed everything, he dried the frame on the hand towel.

Before wrapping up the framed photograph again, he studied it. Charlotte was very, very beautiful. It was outrageous to think that someone thought she was in any way connected with the dirt of the case.

He left and went across to the clerks' room where Marriott gave him some string, which he used to secure the brown paper around the photograph once he was back in his own room. He put the parcel in the centre drawer of his desk, locked the drawer, and dropped the key into his pocket.

* * *

Because the job was almost certainly going to be an extremely unpleasant one, Brock might have been expected to pass it on to one of his subordinates. The detective superintendent was coming down from HQ and his visit was an obvious and perfect excuse. But Brock always carried out the unpleasant tasks that were naturally his because he did not believe that one of the benefits of command was to make others do the dirty work.

As he waited in his car, Squire by his side, Brock wondered whether he should have taken some action while in Holter's room? But what? Any move on his part would merely have resulted in Holter's slamming shut the drawer and refusing to co-operate in any way and he, Brock, could have done nothing about it. Now, in his inside coat pocket, there was a warrant, duly signed, which denied even Radwick Holter his rights as a freeborn citizen.

Detective Constable Squire lit another cigarette. 'That's not at all bad, sir,' he said suddenly.

'What isn't?'

'The bit of skirt coming along. D'you think if I chucked a bob on the pavement, she'd bend down to pick it up?'

Brock was silent.

'The trouble with me, sir, is I'm sex starved.'

'Shut up.'

Squire shut up. He watched the woman go past. It made him sad to think that while men all over the country were chasing beautiful women, he sat in the High Street, slowly being dehydrated by the sun which was turning the DI's rusting old car into an oven.

Brock began to tap his fingers on the steering wheel, but he realized what he was doing and stopped himself. The sense of tension within him was rapidly becoming greater which meant that to some extent Holter had been right when he said that dealing with him was not the same as dealing with some snivelling little pickpocket. Hunches so often went sour. As time passed, they so often seemed more and more like tired flights of fancy.

Then he saw Holter walk out of the building, carrying a small parcel in his right hand.

Brock stepped out of the car and went round the bonnet to the pavement. Squire joined him. 'Mr Holter,' he said, as the latter came abreast of him.

Holter started and stopped abruptly and another pedestrian almost crashed into him. Instinctively, he held the photograph tightly against himself. 'What?'

'Would you mind telling me what's in that parcel?'

Holter looked down at it and shook his head.

'May I see it, please?'

'No.'

Several schoolgirls, in red and white striped blazers, came along the road. Giggling, they split into two groups and swept past on either side of the three men.

'I must ask you to give it to me, sir.'

'How dare you intrude into my privacy like this,' said Holter desperately.

'I have a warrant.'

'A ... a warrant?'

Brocker took the warrant from his pocket and handed it to Holter, who just stared down at the outstretched hand. 'The parcel, please.'

'No.'

'I should hate to have to use force.'

Holter was quite motionless. Brock reached forward and took hold of the parcel. He felt something hard, with a knobbly rim. Using an even, slow force he drew the parcel towards himself. For a second or two Holter resisted, but eventually he let go.

'Would you like to come to my car, sir, so that I can give you a receipt?' asked Brock.

Holter went with the two detectives to the car. Brock

opened the nearside door and sat down sideways on the seat, with his feet on the pavement. He unknotted the string and unwrapped the photograph. He stared down at it. 'Write out the receipt,' he ordered Squire, in a flat voice.

'You can't keep that,' objected Holter.

'Sorry. We'll have to for a while.'

'It's got nothing to do with the murder.'

'Was it in the bottom drawer of your desk?'

'What if it was?'

'Would you tell me why you were so surprised and shocked to find it there?'

'It's none of your business.'

'Very well, sir.'

'I'll crucify you for this.' Holter turned and left, ignoring the receipt that Squire tried to give him.

Brock looked down at the photograph. 'What the hell?'

'I beg your pardon?' said Squire.

'Nothing,' snapped Brock.

* * *

It was thirty hours since Brock had taken the photograph of Charlotte Holter from Radwick Holter. Brock sat at the desk in his room at the central police station and smoked. For something over twenty-nine hours, various high-ranking police officers had been asking whether he realized what he must expect if he had made a mistake. He was beginning to think it more and more likely he had made a mistake. Now, he was sweating it out. The more time that passed, the less likely it was that the photograph held any significance. So Holter had been surprised to find it in his drawer – so what? That didn't go to prove anything and her photograph wasn't suddenly going to start talking.

The telephone rang. Wearily, Brock picked up the receiver. Another irate, worried senior police officer? 'Detective Inspector.'

'There's a call from London for you.'

This was almost certainly the lab report. Was it also, in effect, his obituary as a police officer?

A voice thick with Yorkshire accent said: 'Detective Inspector Brock?'

'Speaking.'

'Lab here, Inspector. About that photograph and frame you sent us.'

'Yes?'

'There's nothing in the photograph, glass, or backing.'

'And the frame?'

'That has its interesting features.'

'What?'

'It has been recently cleaned with soap and water, but not quite well enough. You'll remember the silver is very heavily patterned? Tucked away under one of the scrolls was some dried blood. Not much, mind you, but just enough.'

'Can you type it?'

'Aye.'

'Well?'

'An LV a plus b plus factor.'

Brock remembered Kinnet telling him that that was the make-up of Corry's blood and that it was a pretty piece of research with no relevancy: Kinnet had, for once, been wrong. 'That's Corry's blood.'

'It is, Inspector. Unless one of the fifty other people in the British Isles with that blood happened to be present at the same time.'

'Thanks.'

'Is it going to help?'

'I think so,' replied Brock slowly.

After he had replaced the receiver, Brock leaned back in his chair. Corry's blood had been on the framed photograph of Charlotte Holter. Why had the photograph been in the drawer and not on the desk?

His mind suddenly connected up three things: the bloodied photograph, the trail of blood on the carpet, and the case of *Regina* v Smith.

Albert Smith had clubbed a woman to death, the woman he loved, and as a mad gesture of hatred and repudiation he had dragged her body down to leave it beneath a photograph of himself. Holter had been defending Albert Smith. Corry had been shot and dragged across the carpet to the base of the desk, on which had been the photograph of Charlotte Holter.

Chapter Twelve

HOLTER WAS pathetically bewildered by his arrest: it destroyed his satisfied self-assurance and his will to fight. He was a man who had always believed in the utter rightness of every aspect of the English law and its long traditions and this to a point where it became for him a dogma of his faith: the rules of conduct for members of the Bar were of greater importance than the ten commandments. He knew that, because of the dedication of himself, his fellow counsel, and the judges, the whole of crime detection was geared to only one thing, punishing the guilty and maintaining the freedom of the innocent. Yet, despite the fact that all his professional life had been devoted to supporting this objective, he, an innocent man, was now charged with a murder about which he knew nothing.

The misery of his innocence led him to say ridiculous things. He said he couldn't help in the construction of his own defence. He said that he wouldn't help because he was innocent and only the guilty needed to defend themselves.

Cheesman, Q.C., was briefed to defend Holter – a mixed honour for Cheesman since there would be no brief fee. At the preliminary hearing, he very briefly cross-examined the prosecution witnesses and then reserved his defence. An expected move which only partially hid the fact that he had not yet found how to conduct a worthwhile defence.

There was a consultation in one of the prison conference rooms a few days before the opening of the autumn assizes. Cheesman, his junior, Whits, and Jackley, instructing solicitor, were present. When Holter was escorted into the room by a warder, who retired, everyone was embarrassed.

'Well, Radwick, how are things?' asked Cheesman, with forced cheerfulness.

Holter stared at the other, then slumped down on to one of the free hard wooden chairs.

'Have you got all you want for the moment?'

'I didn't do it,' said Holter dully, 'so how can they charge me?' His naïvety could only be understood when one knew how completely he believed in justice.

Cheesman looked at the others, but they were careful to make it clear that he would have to do all the talking. 'The evidence against you is pretty strong, Radwick.'

'Did you get in touch with all those people?'

'Most of them, yes.'

'What did they say?'

'They expressed real sympathy with you, but said they couldn't possibly interfere with the course of justice.'

There was a silence. Jackley, who had more practical experience than the others of the needs of people on remand, took a packet of cigarettes from his pocket. 'Perhaps you'd like these, Mr Holter?'

Holter stared at the packet for several seconds before he took it. He lit a cigarette. 'I didn't kill Corry. I wasn't there.'

Jackley undid his brief and the two barristers followed suit. The room was filled with the sounds of rustling papers.

'I want first of all to have a word about Mrs Holter,' said Cheesman.

'What about her?' demanded Holter, his voice regaining a little of its old force.

'The prosecution can't call her, of course, since she's your wife. What we've to decide is whether to call her for the defence.'

'Of course we call her.'

'Radwick, we've got to weigh up things really carefully. We mustn't forget that the prosecution evidence that she was in chambers is pretty strong. If we call her to support your evidence, what is going to happen when she's cross-examined?'

'She was never near chambers that night.'

'As Mr Cheesman's just said,' murmured Jackley, 'the evidence against her is rather strong.'

'To hell with the evidence.'

'Let's just look at the admitted facts,' said Cheesman. 'Your wife went to Miss West and asked her to say she'd been there all evening. Yet your wife in fact left the house just before six. Why did she do this and where did she go?'

'She went for a drive and was nowhere near chambers. She was not carrying on some dirty liaison.'

'I'm merely looking at the evidence, Radwick, and trying to treat it on its merits.'

'You don't seem to know what you're bloody well looking at.'

Cheesman stifled any anger he might have felt. 'It wasn't the first time your wife had asked Miss West to say, falsely, that she had been in that house all evening.'

'Rachael West's a liar and she always hated me because I've never tried to hide what I think of her.'

'Look, we must leave that sort of thing alone. Can you tell me why your wife had this arrangement with her?'

'She didn't.'

'Or why she borrowed Miss West's car that Tuesday instead of using her own which was in perfectly good running order?'

'That's another of Rachael's lies.'

'There's independent evidence to the truth of this.'

'Then that's a lie as well.'

'Where did your wife go?'

'Where she says she did: for a drive around the countryside.'

'Very well. Why didn't she use her own car?'

'She did.'

Cheesman sighed as he turned over a sheet of paper. 'A witness testified he saw a woman leaving the building in which your chambers are at a quarter to seven on Tuesday. From his evidence it could only have been your wife.'

'He's either a liar or a short-sighted fool.'

'He's certainly neither and his evidence is going to carry a very great deal of weight with the jury.'

'Charlotte wasn't there.'

'We've got to decide how to handle the evidence of the face powder that was found in your room and which must have got there Tuesday night. Radwick, that powder is so expensive that only a handful of women in Hertonhurst use it and your wife is one of them.'

'There's nothing to say this was Charlotte's.'

'But can't you see that this, together with all the other evidence pointing to her being present...'

'Which the hell side are you on?'

'You know damn' well my one aim is to help you as much as possible.'

'Charlotte wasn't in chambers. Can you understand that? What conceivable reason could there be for her being there?'

'Because she was having an affair with Corry.'

Holter began to swear, with crude repetition. 'She's my wife,' he shouted. 'My wife, d'you understand? She wouldn't even look at another man.'

'It could happen,' said Jackley.

'Not to me it couldn't. Our marriage isn't like that.'

'I'm afraid with the rather great difference in ages...'

'What's that to do with it?'

'The prosecution is going to claim it has a lot to do with it.'

Holter suddenly stood up and kicked his chair away from him. 'Stop your filthy insinuations.'

Cheesman looked at Jackley, who shrugged his shoulders. Whits lit a cigarette. Cheesman turned over several pages of his proof. 'Radwick, the people who were at the dinner at The Three Bells on the Tuesday say you were in a state when you arrived?'

Holter, who had been about to cross to the door, hesitated. 'Well?'

'Were you upset about something?'

Slowly, he sat down once more. After a while, he spoke in a flat voice. 'I'd very nearly been run over. That surely was sufficient reason for being upset?'

'What happened from the moment you left chambers?'

'Corry and I left together. I went one way, when we were outside, and he went the other. I strolled along, thinking, and I was in that road behind the church. It was clear to cross so I started to do so and the next second a car came round the corner at a ridiculous speed. I moved as quickly as I could, but some part of the car touched me and I fell. Yet the car never stopped.'

'It's a pity we've got nothing to help prove that's what happened.'

There was another silence.

Cheesman tapped the end of his silver pencil against his chin. 'Will you tell us how you got the bruise on your neck which the police saw on the Wednesday?'

Holter flushed. 'I've no idea,' he snapped.

* * *

The assize court had been built in the middle thirties. The courtroom was large, airy, and light and it was unusual in that consideration had been given to the comfort of people other than just the judge.

The case of *Regina* v Holter naturally attracted considerable attention and several hundred members of the public queued although warned that only a hundred of them could be admitted. Great difficulty had been experienced in finding a judge to try the case who did not know Holter and, if possible, before whom Holter had never appeared. The legal profession, always jealous of its reputation, was ready to go to any lengths to make certain no one could accuse it of failing rigorously to punish its own wrongdoers. Justice had to be seen to be done more clearly than ever.

Mr Justice Proctor tried the case. He was a man who had never been accused of partiality by anyone, yet neither had anyone ever credited him with a strong sense of humanity. He saw the law as a fence with the innocent on one side and the guilty on the other. After committing a man to prison for several years, he was told the man had just hanged himself. His only comment was that, since suicide was a crime, the man had remained a criminal to the end.

Adems, prosecuting, was a round and tubby figure with a balloon face and a pair of horn rimmed spectacles which he frequently perched at the end of his nose. He opened the case shortly and concisely, dealing at length only with the question of motive.

'Members of the jury, it has frequently been remarked that although motive is so often a vital part of a case of murder, it is in no way an essential one. The prosecution, as a point of law, does not have to prove a motive. In the present case, however, the motive behind the shooting of the dead man can be stated quite simply: it was jealousy. The accused's wife was having an affair with Corry and because of this Corry was shot dead. If you are satisfied these are the facts, you will surely ask yourself: Who had cause to be jealous?

'It may be as well at this point to deal with a question of law, although I am certain his lordship will address you on it in greater detail at some later stage of the trial. Is a husband entitled to escape conviction for murder – but not for manslaughter – if he kills his wife's lover? The answer is clearly established. Should the husband find his wife and her lover *in flagrante delicto* and without pause kills either of them, the provocation is held to be so great that he is not guilty of murder. However, should he pause for any length of time before the act of killing, then he will be guilty of murder and not manslaughter. If the husband finds his wife and lover together in a compromising situation and then goes off to secure a weapon and returns to kill the lover with it, that is murder. That is the law and I shall say no more than that there is no evidence whatsoever that the dead man was caught *in flagrante delicto*.

'Members of the jury, the murderer took from the cabinet on the wall a revolver that was hanging up inside, one of several mementoes of past murder trials. There is this bitterly ironic fact to this case, that the revolver used to kill Corry had already killed twice, and the two empty cartridge cases were still in the chambers together with four live rounds. Members of the jury, I would draw your attention to the several significant facts about this revolver. A casual murderer would surely have believed it to be empty since it was so openly displayed and he would have chosen as his weapon one of the daggers or knives that was in the cabinet. A casual murderer could not have fired this revolver, even had he known it to be loaded, without the greatest difficulty. If the gun is uncocked, it takes a very considerable pressure to pull the trigger: so considerable that experts will tell you that a casual murderer would either be likely to believe the gun was no longer working or else he would take so long that the victim must have time in which to struggle for his life. Yet there was no such struggle. On the other hand, if the gun is cocked, a safety catch is automatically applied, but the safety catch is practically impossible to find by chance or hurried search. Experts, members of the jury, will testify that in their opinion this gun could only have been fired in the circumstances it was by someone who knew precisely how it worked ...'

* * *

Traynton, in the witness-box, was a man of integrity suddenly faced by the need to keep faith with two diametrically opposed duties: he owed an absolute duty both to the law and to Holter.

'You have told us that you arrived at chambers at nine o'clock,' said Adems. 'Will you describe what then happened?'

'I went inside, sir.'

'After unlocking the doors?'

'I found the doors were unlocked, sir.'

'Did that fact cause you to worry?'

'I decided that the last person to leave chambers had been very careless, sir.'

'Did you know who had been the last to leave chambers the previous night?'

'No, sir.'

'To your knowledge, who was there when you left?'

Traynton looked stolidly at the far wall and Adems had to repeat the question. Traynton then, in a voice devoid of inflexion, answered, 'I have no idea, sir.'

Adems stared at the witness over the tops of his glasses. 'As an efficient chief clerk, you must have known who had gone home by the time you left?'

Traynton's ponderous bulk seemed to shiver. 'I ... I was aware that some of the members had departed, sir.'

'Shall we reach the answer by process of elimination? Had Mr Resse said good night to you?'

'Yes, sir.'

'Have you any reason to suppose he didn't leave after speaking to you?'

'No, sir.'

'Had Mr Spender said good night to you and, in so far as you knew, left?'

'Yes, sir.'

'What about Mr Aiden?'

'He had said good night, sir.'

'Did your junior clerk, Mr Marriott, leave before you did?'

'Yes, sir.'

'Was Mrs Fleming with you that afternoon?'

'No, sir.'

'Then will you tell the court who might still have been in chambers other than the accused and the deceased?'

Traynton's expression settled into one of hopeless despair.

'Well, Mr Traynton?'

'There was no one else to my knowledge, sir.'

'When you left chambers there was no one else present other than the accused and the deceased?'

'Yes, sir. But someone might have come in without my knowing.'

'Is that a common occurrence?'

Traynton was silent.

'Shall we return to events which we know took place? On the following morning, that is Wednesday the sixteenth of July, you found on your arrival that the two outer doors were unlocked and you naturally assumed that the last person to leave chambers had been very careless. Whom did you believe had been careless?'

'I...I...'

'Was it not Mr Holter?'

Cheesman without bothering to rise, objected: 'You can't cross-examine. He is your witness, you know.'

Adems momentarily smiled. 'I beg leave to doubt that.' When it was clear the judge was going to say nothing, he addressed the witness again. 'What happened next?'

'I went into my room, sir, sorted through the mail and distributed it.'

'Did anything unusual happen?' asked Adems, with mild sarcasm.

'There was a man lying on the floor of Mr Holter's room, sir. It was clear he was very badly injured so I returned to the clerks' room and telephoned Mr Holter.'

'Why?'

'Naturally, to tell him what had happened, sir.'

'Don't you think it would have been more correct to have contacted the police first?'

'They are Mr Holter's chambers.'

'And he had been in them when you left the previous night,' murmured Adems, as he turned a page of his proof.

Cheesman stood up. 'My lord, I really must object. My learned friend has absolutely no right to try to imply what he has done.'

'Quite so, Mr Cheesman,' answered the judge blandly. 'I fully agree that this is an inference for the jury to draw.'

Out-manoeuvred, and not wishing to give the judge room for further comment, Cheesman sat down.

Traynton stared over the heads of the jury in the hopes that by doing so he could disassociate himself from what was going on. He had always said that Mr Holter was not a gentleman: the fact that Mr Holter was now a prisoner on trial, publicly guarded by a warder, most bitterly showed how true that was.

* * *

Marriott, who followed Traynton into the box, tried to remain as cockily certain of everything as usual and failed. Years of intimate association with the courts had not prepared him for the loneliness of the witness-box.

Adems removed his spectacles and polished them on the edge of his gown. 'Will you tell the court, to the best of your ability, what was normally on top of the accused's desk?'

'Papers and things.'

'What things?'

'You know, the usual kind of things.'

'Whether counsel does, or does not, know is not the point,' said the judge sharply. 'He has asked you a question and you will answer it to the best of your ability.'

Marriott hastily spoke in a very subdued manner. 'There was a presentation ink-well, pencils, a blotter, and the photo.'

'What photograph is this?'

'Of his wife.'

'Will you please look at exhibit number seven and say whether you recognize it?'

The usher picked up the framed photograph from the

table in front of the Bench and carried it to the witness-box. 'That's it,' said Marriott.

'And you would expect to find this on the accused's desk?'

'It always was there.'

'Can you ever remember its not being there?'

'D'you mean before or after?'

'Before the murder.'

'No, never.'

'What about afterwards?'

'It wasn't there.'

'Did you notice its absence at the time?'

'Couldn't help noticing that it wasn't there.'

'Have you seen it at any time between the night of the murder and now?'

'No.'

'Were you ever asked if you knew where it had gone to?'

'No, sir, never.'

The examination of Marriott continued for another half-hour and then Adems sat down. After leaning forward and speaking to his solicitor, Cheesman stood up. 'No questions,' he said.

The public were clearly surprised, mistakenly imagining that every prosecution witness would be severely cross-examined. After the murmur of conversation had died away, the judge looked at the clock and adjourned the court for lunch.

Chapter Thirteen

THE WEALD TOWN of Brackensham, the inhabitants of which were once threatened by wholesale excommunication when they refused with typical Kentish vigour to heed the commands of Pope Gregory the 12th, was a town which during assizes dined all members of the Bar and higher court officials. It was a welcome custom for counsel, some of whom could not have afforded to have eaten half as well, and there was no undue burden on the ratepayers who, in any case, knew practically nothing about it.

During the luncheon on the first day of the Holter trial, Adems sat between the clerk of the assize and Cheesman. A waiter refilled all their glasses with a 1963 Beaune that one of the councillors had found very difficult to sell in his chain of wineshops.

Adems lifted his glass and drank. 'There's a nasty taste to it all, isn't there?'

'A bit corked?' suggested the clerk of assize.

'No, no. I meant seeing old Holter in the dock. He's been offered a judgeship at least once and turned it down. It throws a smell over the whole of the profession.'

'Aren't you presuming the verdict?' asked Cheesman.

Adems cut in half the remaining piece of steak on his plate. 'Care to put your reputation on a verdict of not guilty?'

Cheesman shrugged his shoulders.

'The moral's obvious,' said the clerk of assize. 'Old men, however sexy they feel, shouldn't marry young women.'

'He's not all that old,' objected Cheesman.

'Sorry. Didn't realize I was treading on delicate ground.'

'D'you know Mrs Holter?' asked Adems.

'I've seen her more than once. If you ask me to speak freely, I say she's a bitch: not that I don't find bitches attractive. My wife reckons she ought to be on trial, but wives hate their own sex, given the chance.'

'If only Radwick Holter hadn't got so worked up about things. A quick divorce would have done just as well and saved all this.'

'There's no fool like an old fool.'

'He's not all that old,' snapped Cheesman.

* * *

At the beginning of the trial, Holter had listened to proceedings in a totally apathetic mood. This quickly gave way to one of professional criticism and as soon as this happened he was shocked by a realisation, however belated, of the strength of the prosecution's case. He was mentally staggered by the extent to which the evidence damned him and all too easily he was able to gauge how readily the jury would believe Charlotte had been in chambers at the time of the murder.

Back in his cell during the lunch adjournment, he ate the food they gave him without being really aware of what it was. As soon as he had finished, he began to pace the few feet of the floor. He tried to ignore the steel door, the lack of an inside handle, the bars over the windows, the iron bunk, and the stained lavatory bowl, but they all seemed to close in on him. Often, he had visited men in cells, but this was the first time he had understood how small a cell was.

He lit a cigarette. If he were found guilty he would lose Charlotte, an unbearable thought. He stood still. Charlotte was twenty-six and no one could expect her to live the life of a recluse in the future. She would meet another man with whom she would fall in love, perhaps marry, go to bed with. The thought of her in bed with another man filled his mind with bitter anger. He began to imagine her, naked, and this unknown man, naked, and he swore crudely. Seconds later, he saw a movement at the spy hole and he knew, with a sudden surge of violent revulsion, that he was being watched.

He thought of his brothers and sisters who still lived in or around Ashby-de-la-Zouch. They had envied him for years because he had everything anyone could want, money and success: in return, he had been contemptuous of them because they had not had the ability or the gumption to drag themselves clear of the sticks. Now he envied them because they were free, and they must think of him with contempt.

He must prove his innocence: the facts must be made to wear their true face. Until now, he had stubbornly believed that the truth would rise to the surface as an act of natural justice, but now he saw that it needed to be kicked up. Cheesman must kick and kick: he must fight every inch of the way: he must cross-examine exhaustively, even brutally until at last the truth was told.

The cell door opened and a warder stepped inside. 'All ready, sir. They'll be back in court in a jiffy.'

As he left the cell, he thought how odd it was that they still called him 'Sir,' as if the shreds of the dignity of freedom still clung to him.

* * *

After the adjournment, Doctor Kinnet was called into the witness-box, looking even thinner than usual because of the colour and cut of the suit he was wearing. A 'professional' witness, the second oldest profession in the world he called it, he gave his evidence concisely and accurately.

'Doctor Kinnet,' said Adems, 'Will you please tell the court if it's possible to say whether, or not, the deceased died immediately?'

'It's impossible to be certain that the deceased made no voluntary physical movement after he was shot, but the damage to the brain was so extensive that I would hold it to be highly improbable.'

The judge spoke. 'Doctor, would you deem it possible that the deceased, after being shot, crawled from the cabinet to the desk?'

'My lord, I would consider it next to impossible, but I am not prepared to say that it was impossible. By this I mean that if there was other proof suggesting this is what did happen, the wound he suffered would not automatically negative such evidence.'

'Had he died immediately and been dragged from the one point to the other, what would you expect the medical evidence to be?'

'A trail of blood, similar to the one I was shown on the carpet.'

'Thank you.' The judge wrote in his note-book.

Adems adjusted the set of his wig and flicked the tails clear of his thick neck. 'What conclusions did you reach, Doctor, concerning the death of the deceased?'

'I examined for powder-tattooing and blacking about the wound and for powder stains on both hands. There weren't any. I carried out experiments with the murder weapon and with ammunition of similar make and age. From these experiments, I decided that the gun was fired at a distance of not less that fifteen inches – that is, the muzzle was fifteen inches from the point of entry of the bullet.

'I then reconstructed the shooting by examining the line the shot had taken. I finally reached the conclusion that the deceased did not commit suicide.'

'Could you further detail the reasons for this decision?'

'Suicide by shooting is almost invariably carried out by pressing the muzzle of the gun against the skin on one of the classical sites of election, as they're called. These are the right temple, for right-handed people, the centre brow, the roof of the mouth, and the heart. The would-be suicide does not wish to miss himself or hit a non-vital area. In this case, the gun was held at least fifteen inches away from the head and the point of entry of the bullet was behind the right ear. If you reconstruct this position you will see that it is inconceivable that any person would commit suicide thus.'

'Thank you.'

The examination-in-chief continued, slowly, carefully, inexorably.

Cheesman's cross-examination was brief. 'Doctor, you told my learned friend that you carried out certain experiments to ascertain the distance at which the gun was fired. What was the nature of these experiments?'

'I used the murder gun to fire bullets into various substances.'

'Including human flesh?'

'Yes.'

'Of dead people?'

'There were no living volunteers.'

Cheesman's voice sharpened. 'Is it not a fact, Doctor, that dead flesh responds to such experiments in a different manner from live flesh? Tattooing on live skin will not be exactly reproduced by controlled experiments on dead skin?'

'That is so.'

'Then when you say the muzzle of the gun must have been at least fifteen inches from the skin, you are basing such argument on admittedly erroneous premises? Wouldn't it be better to stick to the facts, rather than try to bias the jury by figures which we now learn may mean nothing?'

'Well, now, I don't think that's quite accurate. The possibility of error in the circumstances outlined is generally held to be of the order of five per cent. If my mental arithmetic isn't too rusty, that gives a figure for this case of three-quarters of an inch. Suppose we take the minimum figure and not the maximum one and the gun was held fourteen and a quarter inches from the skin – I don't think that really invalidates my original contention.'

Cheesman tried to hide the fact that he had been led into an error of cross-examination by continuing to attack the witness. 'It would have been better, Doctor, to have declared the possibility of an error at the beginning.'

The doctor said nothing.

'You have stated that this was not a case of suicide. Can you tell us whether the gun was fired at a distance of sixteen or sixty inches?'

'No, I cannot.'

'Somebody on the other side of the room in chambers might have been handling the gun and it went off accidentally?'

'Medically, I know of no reason why not.'

'Or the deceased might have been holding the gun more than sixteen inches away from his head and it went off accidentally?'

'Solely on the evidence of the lack of tattooing, yes.'

Cheesman sat down.

Adems re-examined. 'Doctor, you examined the deceased's hands for powder residue and found them negative. What does this mean?'

'I carried out tests with this revolver. Normally, it leaves powder stains on the hand that fires it and normally those stains can be shown to exist. Because there was none on the deceased's hands, I think it unlikely that he fired a gun that day.'

'How unlikely?'

'Very unlikely.'

'But not impossible?'

'No, not impossible.'

'Have you had much experience of accidental gun wounds?'

'I have seen a reasonable number.'

'Can you ever recall an accidental wound at an angle similar to the angle in this case?'

'No. As I have already said, the point of entry was behind the right ear, at an angle of one hundred and twenty degrees.' The doctor raised his right hand and then bent it back so that his wrist was roughly at the indicated angle. 'It is difficult even to get the hand back this far,' he said.

'And even more difficult if that hand is holding a gun?' said the judge. 'Doctor, in your considered opinion, taking into account all the facts known to you, was Corry shot by his own hand or the hand of another?'

'The hand of another, my lord.'

* * *

Police witnesses gave their evidence. Brock went into the witness-box and for an hour and a half was examined-in-chief. At the end of this time, he was cross-examined.

'I want to deal with the locks on the two outer doors of chambers. You have testified, Inspector, that in your opinion they were not forced.'

'Yes, sir.'

'Can you be certain beyond any reasonable doubt whatsoever that an expert thief did not force those locks, yet left no trace of what he had done?'

'Yes, sir.'

'Your confidence is absolute?'

'In my professional career I have examined a very great number of locks which have been forced and in every single case there have been marks.'

'Suppose we confine ourselves to discussing the work of expert lock-pickers?'

'Most lock-pickers consider themselves experts.'

'You are determined to have it your way, Inspector. Can you assure the court that it is impossible that someone obtained the keys for long enough to have them copied and then used this second set?'

'I've checked as far as possible and there's no record of any of the keys having been mislaid.'

'But this could have happened without any record and such keys could have been used? And these keys would have left no marks in the locks?'

'I suppose so, sir.'

'You don't wish to admit you may have been over-confident?'

'I was just thinking how unlikely it was.'

'That remark is totally uncalled for,' snapped Cheesman.

'Uncalled for,' murmured the judge, 'but quite understandable.'

Cheesman chose not to hear the judge. 'You have testified, Inspector, that there are no signs of a struggle?'

'That's correct.'

'But surely even you will admit there could have been either a struggle in which no visible signs were left or a struggle after which all visible signs were erased?'

'Not in my opinion, sir.'

'Why not?'

'Any sort of a prolonged struggle, sir, leaves traces. Any attempt to erase those traces inevitably leaves further traces.'

'But the prosecution can't have it both ways. They are claiming that the bruises on the accused's throat, about which you've given evidence, were gained in a struggle.'

'I can't speak on that score, sir.'

'The accused could suffer bruising on the throat from one blow, Mr Cheesman. That can hardly be termed a struggle,' said the judge, 'even by counsel for the defence.'

Cheesman, never before so conscious of trying to defend without a defence, silently cursed. 'You have said, Inspector, that you searched the room and found powder on the carpet?'

'Yes.'

'You sent the powder for analysis. Before we go any further, will you tell the court how you know that this powder was not spilled on the carpet several days prior to the Tuesday in question?'

'All the evidence I was able to gather led me to this definite assumption.'

'Your evidence is based on assumptions, not facts?'

Adems rose and took off his spectacles. 'My lord, it may assist my learned friend to know that the prosecution is calling evidence to show that the powder was not on the carpet prior to the Tuesday evening.'

'My lord,' replied Cheesman, 'I think it should be made quite clear to the jury that the inspector does not know this of his own account.'

'He has never claimed that he does,' said the judge.

Adems sat down. Cheesman leaned forward to read part of his brief. After a while, he stood up. 'This powder was indentified as Drage three two five and your investigations show that only one chemist in Hertonhurst stocks it and that only about five customers buy it?'

'Yes, sir.'

'There are, I suppose you will admit, other towns in Kent? Some of them are quite a bit bigger than Hertonhurst?'

'That is why we got a list from the manufacturers of the retailers who stock their products.'

'And this list was quite a long one?'

'Yes, sir.'

'Then obviously a number of women in Kent use Drage three two five face powder?'

'The best estimate we can make is about two hundred.'

'And there are other counties in England?'

The judge sighed audibly. 'Mr Cheesman, are we now about to examine *seriatim* the statistics for each of the other thirty-nine counties in England?'

'My lord, surely I am entitled to show the lack of worth of this evidence?'

'You are certainly entitled to try, but I trust at not too great a length.'

'Inspector,' snapped Cheesman, 'is it not a fact that in the whole of England there must be thousands of women who use this particular face powder?'

'We only concerned ourselves with Kent, sir.'

Cheesman turned over a page of his brief. His junior, Whits, tugged the back of his gown to draw his attention and then handed him a note. He read it and nodded. He addressed the witness again. 'I want to turn now to the photograph you claim was in the bottom drawer of the accused's desk. The accused is going to say ...'

The cross-examining continued.

* * *

The court adjourned at four thirty-three and Holter was escorted down the steps at the back of the dock to the passage below and along to the cells. He was told that at six o'clock he would be taken back to the jail.

Once alone, he lit a cigarette. His brain seemed to be about to explode from the frightening sense of tortured impotence. The jaws of justice were closing around him and there seemed to be nothing to prevent their crushing him. He was innocent, yet his innocence was his greatest danger. Actions which at the time had been perfectly normal had become the actions of guilt.

He had not been in chambers that Tuesday night, yet the evidence was saying that he had and that he had shot Corry: Charlotte had not been near chambers that Tuesday night, yet the evidence was saying that she had and that Corry had been her lover. How could evidence be so wrong?

What was that bitch, Rachael West, going to say in the witness-box? If she testified that Charlotte had frequently borrowed her car and driven off somwhere when officially she was at Rachael's house, what were people going to think? 'Oh, God!' he cried aloud. He knew Charlotte through and through: she couldn't descend to anything so sordid as an affair. But how was he going to make others understand that?

The cell door opened and a warder said that his lawyers wanted a word with him. Seconds later, Cheesman, Whits, and Jackley came in. The steel door shut with a clang that shivered the soul.

All his fears came welling out. 'Why aren't you attacking the witnesses more?'

Cheesman, a worried expression on his face, looked quickly at Jackley.

'You've got to fight. Fight, d'you hear? You let the detective inspector get away with everything.'

The newcomers sat down, Cheesman and Whits on the bunk and Jackley on the chair.

'It's a difficult case, Radwick,' said Cheesman.

'You can't damn' well tell me anything about it I don't know.'

'There's a pile of evidence against us.'

Holter crossed the floor until he stood immediately in

front of the bunk. 'I'm innocent. I wasn't near chambers and Charlotte wasn't either. The evidence is all goddamn lies. You've got to attack.'

'Radwick, you must leave the handling of the case to me. I'm the best judge of what course to take.'

The attempt to pacify him by using a formula he had so often spoken to his own clients angered Holter even more. 'I've left it all to you and where in the hell has it got me?'

'It's far too early to say.'

'Maybe it's far too early for you, but it isn't for me. I'm looking at a convicted murderer when I stare into a mirror. If I'd been handling the defence the cross-examination of the inspector would have been a hell of a sight more effective.'

'We don't all conduct a defence alike, Radwick.'

'No, by God! we don't, more's the pity. You've let the judge get away with everything.'

Cheesman allowed a little of his anger to show. 'In my opinion, it does not pay to bandy words with a judge.'

'And in mine it does, when the bloody fool shows the partiality Proctor's showing. If you don't stand up to him, the jury will think you haven't a case.'

'They could just be right.'

Holter's voice rose. 'Do you believe I shot Corry?'

Cheesman was about to answer when Jackley hastily intervened. 'It must be a little difficult,' he said, with all the smooth tact he could muster, 'for you, Mr Holter, to have to watch someone else conduct the defence.'

'Damned difficult and unrewarding.'

'Every man has his own methods.'

'And most of them are wrong.'

'I really can assure you we're doing our very best for you.'

'Maybe, but I happen to be intimately concerned with just how effective your best is. I was the last one to leave chambers and Corry was with me, but we separated in the street and I went one way and he went the other. That's all I know about anything.'

'There was a woman present,' said Cheesman.

'If there was, she wasn't Charlotte.'

'But we can't ignore the evidence of that eye-witness,

Wallace. He saw a woman leave the building and from the description of her clothes it could only have been your wife.'

'She wasn't there.'

'Radwick, it's doing far more harm than good to go on ignoring the facts. . . .'

'The facts are, she wasn't there. She wasn't bloody well there.'

Cheesman shrugged his shoulders. 'All right,' he muttered. There was a long pause before he spoke again. 'Let's get onto this trail of blood. It's certain the body was dragged across to the desk. Can you suggest any reason for this unless it was to dump the body under the photograph of your wife?'

'A thousand and one reasons.'

'That the jury will swallow? Radwick, can't you see . . . Never mind. Why did you hide that photograph of your wife?'

'I didn't. I found it in the bottom drawer.'

'Then why didn't you tell the inspector about it?'

'Well, I . . . I supposed I panicked.'

'Innocent men don't panic.'

'This one bloody well did. The moment I saw the blood on the frame I remembered the trail of blood. It was obvious someone had tried to suggest I'd shot Corry and dragged the body across.'

'Wouldn't this person have left the photo on top of the desk where it would be bound to draw the attention of the police?'

'That's just what he didn't do, did he?'

'But that's the obvious question the jury are going to ask. You then tried to smuggle the photo out of chambers.'

'I didn't want anyone to start getting the same kind of idea as I had.'

'That's not much of an explanation for the jury.'

'Hang the jury.'

'It'll pay you to remember the boot's on the other foot.'

'I'm not having anyone say Charlotte was in chambers with that gigolo.'

There was another pause.

Whits whispered to Cheesman, who spoke to Holter.

'Suppose that trail of blood was made to try to incriminate you? Any idea who would have done such a thing?'

'D'you think I'd allow myself to be shut up here if I could answer?'

'It would have to be someone from chambers.'

'No one in chambers would do such a thing.'

'But somebody did.' Cheesman stood up and the other two followed suit. Jackley knocked on the door of the cell. 'We'll see you tomorrow,' said Cheesman.

The door was opened by the warder. Cheesman led the way outside.

Just before the cell door was slammed shut, Holter thought he heard Cheesman refer to the impossibility of helping a sick doctor who insisted on making his own faulty diagnosis and prognosis. Holter paced the cell floor. Anger and fear flooded through his mind, but they didn't obscure one essential fact: truth was proving to be a liar and was squeezing the life out of him. When truth was a liar, where did one turn?

* * *

It was midnight. Holter lay in his cell in the prison and listened to the noises outside. He heard the measured tread of a warder, a shout from somewhere that was repeated once, and the almost continuous knocking from the next cell whose sole occupant was said to be mad.

When truth was a liar, man was impotent. The world ceased to be. Unless ... unless a lie became the truth.

Chapter Fourteen

HOLTER, STILL technically innocent, was allowed several 'privileges' which would cease the moment he was found guilty. One of these was his right to see his legal advisers during the course of the trial at any reasonable time of the day. On the morning of the second day, he asked to see his solicitor as early as the latter could get to prison.

Breakfast was brought to his cell by a trusty who whiningly asked for a cigarette. Without thinking about what he was doing, he passed across a three-quarters full packet and it was only after the cell door had been shut and locked that he realized he now had none for himself.

He ate his breakfast, careless about how it tasted. All his faculties were intent on only one thing, trying to remember every piece of evidence given the previous day.

Immediately he had finished eating, he lay on the bunk and, as he stared at the ceiling, mentally reviewed all the evidence. Could he get away with it?

Jackley arrived at eight forty-five and Holter was speaking to him before he was properly inside the interview-room. 'I'm taking over my own defence.'

Jackley crossed to the table and put down his brief-case. He sat down and brought out some papers. 'Is that very wise?'

'I wouldn't be doing it if I didn't think so.'

'Even in your case it's not a course I can suggest. Any accused man in naturally totally involved in his own case and he needs to be represented by someone who can remain apart....'

'I'm not remaining anywhere, to watch the lot of you make a mess of things.'

Jackley struggled to retain a degree of pleasantness. 'I'm sure we've all been doing our best....'

'Which hasn't been nearly good enough. I want you to get in touch with my wife and ask her to come and see me as soon as she can.'

'I don't know that that's possible.'

'Then make it so.' Holter had regained much of his former belligerence and bombast.

* * *

Almost to his own amazement, Jackley was able to arrange a meeting between Charlotte and Radwick Holter. Half an hour before the court was due to sit, Charlotte and Jackley were shown into the cell beneath the courtroom into which Holter had earlier been transferred. Jackley, who had expected to be present during the consultation, was rudely ordered out.

Charlotte shivered as the cell door clanged shut.

Holter stared at her, trying visually to appreciate all the beauty that for so many days had been only in his memory. He longed to run his hands through her blonde hair, to hold her close to himself. 'Hullo, darling,' he said hoarsely.

'Hullo, Radwick,' she answered, almost in a whisper.

'I've been worrying myself sick about you.'

'I've ... I've been terrified for you, Radwick. It's been so lonely at home. I keep looking for you and you're not there.'

'I soon will be.'

'Isn't the case ... Isn't it difficult?'

He laughed. 'Surely you're not like the rest of 'em? Forgetting I'm the best criminal lawyer at the Bar?'

'But it all seems so hopeless.'

'Never.' His tone of voice changed and some of the bluster went out of it. 'Sit down, Betty.'

He watched her sit down on the bunk. Her skirt rode up from her knees. The sight of just a little of her upper leg was enough to make his throat go dry, yet he knew every inch of her legs. He sat down. 'I want you to do something to help me escape prison.'

She fiddled with the gloves she was carrying.

'It means asking a lot of you.'

She looked quickly at him and then away. 'What?'

For the first time, he was uncertain of himself. He went to speak, but stopped. Then the words came in a rush. 'I want you to give some evidence in court and say you were in chambers when Corry was shot.'

She gasped.

He moved forward until he could take hold of her right hand.

She jerked her hand free. 'No,' she said, shrilly.

'It's to help me go free.'

'I won't. I won't. I swear I wasn't there.'

'I know you weren't.'

'Then you can't ask me to do such a thing.'

'Darling, it's the only chance I have.'

'What are you trying to do to me?'

'You must understand that if this case goes on as it is now I'm going to be found guilty. Then what will happen to you? We haven't saved anything since we got married.'

'Whose fault is that? You've always said it wasn't necessary. You told me to spend all I wanted to.'

'Of course I did, because I loved seeing you spend money. But what I'm saying is that if I can't earn any more, there won't be much for you.'

'Radwick, you don't really think I was there, do you?'

She took hold of his hand which she had so recently thrust away from herself. 'Promise me you don't think that.'

'I don't for a second.'

'Then how can you want me to say I was in the room?'

'I'm trying to explain why.'

'Radwick, I'm terrified you may have begun to doubt me. All the time I've been at home I've imagined you, thinking. But I promise you that I was just driving round the country lanes. I only borrowed Rachael's car because there seemed to be something wrong with my Merc.'

'My dearest, stop torturing yourself like this. It wouldn't matter what anyone said, how many filthy lies they told, I wouldn't begin to doubt you. I love you, Betty, and I know you've always told me the truth.'

'But I can't say I was there.'

He eased his hand free of hers and stood up. He paced the floor twice and then came to a stop. 'I know what it means to you, but I promise you there just isn't any other way. Try to keep on telling yourself how much you'll be helping me. Look, this is what I'm going to do. I'll prove you were in chambers that night by using all the lies the prosecution have dredged up. Can you see the wonderful irony in this? When they realize what I'm doing they won't be able to take any avoiding action because they can't turn round and try to deny their own lies.'

'Please ... please don't make me do it.'

'I promise you it won't be that bad.'

She ran her tongue along her lips. She shivered again as

she had when she first entered the cell. For once, she looked considerably older than she really was.

Holter paced the cell once more.

*   *   *

As was the custom at Brackensham Assizes, the arrival in court of the judge each morning was heralded by a trumpet fanfare, played by members of the Kentish Yeomen Light Infantry, in their dress uniforms in bottle green. Mr Justice Proctor, who hated trumpets, waited with scant patience until the noise was over and the trumpeters had left the dais and then he briefly returned counsel's bows and sat down.

Adems stood up. 'My lord...'

'One moment, Mr Adems.' The judge spoke to his clerk who left the dais by the door. 'Yes?'

'My lord, I think you should know immediately that the accused has decided to represent himself for the rest of the trial.'

Waiting till the buzz of comment had died down, the judge turned and spoke to Holter in the dock. 'Is that so?'

'Yes, my lord.'

The judge pressed his thin lips tightly together and scratched his long, thin chin. 'Normally, in such an event, I make perfectly certain that the accused realizes the seriousness of the step he proposes to take. In my experience, no prisoner can conduct his case better than his counsel, provided such counsel is of even moderate intelligence and ability. You clearly need no words from me to explain your position, nevertheless I ask you to reconsider your proposal.'

'I don't need to, my lord.'

The judge's expression seemed to become even sourer. 'Very well. But let one thing be abundantly clear. An accused person who chooses to defend himself is often allowed considerable latitude with regard to the rules of evidence. There will be no such latitude in this instance.'

'That's quite all right,' said Holter, as if conferring a favour.

The trial was resumed. Three witnesses gave evidence which was really formal in nature and those who had expected verbal fireworks from Holter were disappointed. His cross-examination was perfunctory.

Edward Wallace was called. He was a small man with a loud voice and a belligerent manner. Adems put the preliminary questions to him and he answered them in a voice filled with self-assurance.

'Mr Wallace, do you remember Tuesday, the fifteenth of July?'

'I'll say I do.'

'Where were you on that day?'

'In Hertonhurst. I works in the bakery.'

'What are your hours of work?'

'Most days I start at five in the morning and carry on to three-thirty in the afternoon. It's half-day on Wednesdays.'

'What hours did you work on this Tuesday?'

'Same as I've just said. I packed up near enough to three-thirty.'

'What did you do then?'

'Went and saw my brother what lives in south Hertonhurst and ain't been very well. I left his place some time after six and caught a bus back to the centre of the town and just missed the connection so I decided to walk home, on account of it not being far. I was just passing the place where all them lawyers work....'

'Can you tell us what time this was?'

'A quarter to seven. The church clock was striking.'

'Did you know then what building it was you were passing?'

'No, but it was in all the papers next day and I recognized it.'

'Thank you. Please carry on.'

'Well, a woman come running out of the building. In a terrible state, she was. I could see she was in a terrible state.'

'Were you able to see her face?'

'Couldn't see much of it, no. But it was the way she was acting, all nervous and scared, like. Couldn't be no mistake.'

Adems silently cursed the witness who was elaborating his evidence to increase its importance. The more he elaborated, the more open he would be to cross-examination and few people could as destructively cross-examine as Holter.

'Will you please confine yourself to the facts,' he said sharply.

'She was upset and no mistake and that's a fact.'

'You have told us you could not see much of her face. Can you otherwise describe her?'

'She was wearing a pink frock with a front that near gave me a heart attack.'

'What does this witness mean?' said the judge angrily, as he dropped his pencil on to the desk.

'It plunged,' said Wallace hurriedly. 'It plunged in the front like it was never going to stop.'

'Can you tell us anything more about it?' asked Adems.

'There weren't no belt and it was a very tight fit.'

'You have said it was pink. What kind of pink?'

'A nice bright one.'

'Did you notice anything else about this woman?'

'She had blonde hair, real blonde. With her dress, it made me think of strawberries and cream, not that cream's really that colour, is it?'

'Anything more?'

'Her shoes were the same colour as her frock and so was her handbag: proper symphony, she was. Even the buttons was the same.'

'Were you asked by the police to look at a number of different photographs to see if you could identify this woman?'

'A copper comes along with a whole stack of 'em, yes.'

'With what result?'

'I recognized one of 'em.'

'Was the photograph the one that the usher will now show you?' The usher handed the witness a photograph. 'Exhibit number forty-one, my lord.'

'That's her,' said Wallace.

'My lord,' said Adems, 'evidence will be given that this is a photograph of Mrs Charlotte Holter.' He addressed the witness again. 'I want you to be utterly frank. Are you positive beyond any doubt that the woman in this photograph is the woman you saw in the High Street, bearing in mind that you have testified you could not see much of her face?'

'No doubt at all.'

Adems hesitated, but decided that he must leave the defence to do whatever they wanted with this witness who was so patently over-confident. He sat down.

All the lawyers present knew that what must follow would be a bitterly destructive cross-examination. Wallace had proved to be a sitting target for anyone of Holter's calibre.

Holter stood up and came to the front of the dock. He reached up to the right-hand side of his head, as if adjusting a wig. Conscious he was the centre of all attention, he looked slowly from the witness to the jury and then back at the witness. 'No questions.' He stepped back to his chair and sat down.

For several seconds there was a silence, as if no one could believe Holter had refused to cross-examine, then the noise of excited conversation rose.

The usher called for silence, a cry taken up by the police. Eventually, there was silence.

The judge rested his elbows on the desk and leaned forward slightly. 'Mr Holter, I feel it my duty to remind you that if you do not challenge the evidence which has just been given now, you may not do so later.'

'Quite so.'

'Very well,' snapped the judge.

The witness left the stand.

* * *

The case for the prosecution was completed in the middle of the morning of the third day. The judge asked Holter whether he was addressing the court, giving evidence, and calling witnesses.

'My lord, I do not propose to open, but I shall myself give evidence and shall then call one witness.'

'Before you do so, I wish to make quite certain that you continue to refuse to be represented by counsel? I feel I should be forgoing my duty if I did not point out to you yet again that had you retained the services of Mr Cheesman and his junior, you would now have the unbiased and expert advice of which you may well have great need.'

'My lord, I consider my own biased and expert advice to be more than adequate.'

The judge did not answer in case he said something he would instantly regret.

Holter left the dock and, accompanied by a warder, went into the witness-box and took the oath. He faced the jury.

'On Tuesday, the fifteenth of July, I left chambers just before six o'clock in the evening. When I said I was going, Corry asked if he might stay on and try to look up a point of law in the case books. I said he might. Because I was giving an after-dinner speech, I did as I usually do and walked along the roads without worrying where I was going, composing the speech in my mind. By pure chance, I returned along the High Street just as my wife walked across the pavement and into the building in which were chambers.'

With a sense of theatrical timing, Holter stopped talking. He looked at the jury for several seconds. When he next spoke, his voice was low and solemn. 'Thinking she must be looking for me, I followed her into the building, went up the stairs, and along to chambers. Both doors were unlocked and I went inside. I heard the sound of voices from my own room so I crossed to the door. Corry was trying to make passionate love to my wife. At first I was too upset and astounded to do anything, then I went into the room.

'Corry was trying to kiss my wife and she was struggling to free herself. He saw me and was so shocked that he let go of her. She was even more shocked and, not knowing what she was doing, she ran out of the room. I was mad with rage and I rushed at him, desperate to hurt him. But, members of the jury, as you can all too plainly see I am not cast in the mould of a superman. I'm overweight and under-exercised. Corry was younger, fitter, and stronger than me. He thrust me aside with humiliating ease, hitting me on my throat which is how I got the bruise. I fell to the ground and lay there, unable to do anything, whilst he jeered at me for being so weak. I dragged myself to my feet and cursed him and, I suppose to try to cover his embarrassment, he pretended he was terrified of my curses. He begged me not to kill him; safe in his own strength he mocked me by pretending that only my inaction would save him. I was silent and he increased his savage mockery. He went to the cabinet on the wall and pulled out the revolver and said he'd have defended himself with that if only it were loaded. I demanded to know why he was trying to break up my marriage. He expressed bitter contrition for what he'd done and swore that he'd show me how remorseful he was. He pressed the muzzle of the gun against his left breast and said that if only he'd got a bullet and the courage, he'd shoot himself to prove that my marriage meant far more to him than his life. I was silent. He became angry. He asked me what I expected from life when I was too old for my wife and she obviously needed someone younger to wear her out. Those were his words, members of the jury. To wear her out. He played the fool again and said that if I really wouldn't give him the balm of forgiveness, he'd have to commit suicide to atone for his cruelty. He aimed the gun at his head and tried to pull the trigger, but couldn't. He said the gun wouldn't work so that he was denied atonement. I told him it worked if it was cocked. He roared with laughter as he cocked the gun. When he tried to pull the trigger, nothing happened. He made out it was obvious the gods didn't mean him to sacrifice himself. I told him it wasn't the gods, it was the safety catch. He asked me where it was and how it worked. I told him. He released the safety catch, held the gun at arm's length and pointed it at his head. He turned his head to look straight at me, jeered at me once more, said, "It is a far, far better thing I do,' and pulled the trigger. He fell to the ground.

'My wife ran into the room and when she saw him on the ground she believed I had shot him. She was far too hysterical for me to explain the truth to her, but I managed to get her out of the room. I was about to leave when I saw the photograph of her on the desk and I suddenly had the insane idea of dragging the body up to the desk to show the same sort of contempt for the dead man as had the murderer in the case I had defended some time earlier. I dragged the body along the carpet and it wasn't until then that I realized just how crazy a thing I'd done and how the police must immediately realize the significance of the trail of blood and believe I had killed Corry. That's why I had the photograph in the bottom drawer of my desk.

'I went out of the room and as soon as my wife was sufficiently in control of herself, I persuaded her to leave.

I followed her ten minutes later. She has lied about certain facts from that day to this because I have never been able to convince her I didn't shoot Corry and she's been trying to defend me.'

The judge spoke. 'You were well aware that the revolver contained four live cartridges?'

'I was.'

'On your own testimony, you allowed him to point this loaded gun first at his heart and then at his head?'

'I did.'

'You knew he believed it to be unloaded?'

'Yes.'

'You knew equally well it was a ridiculous jest when he said he wanted to commit suicide?'

'Yes.'

'Yet you encouraged him to pull the trigger?'

'I merely did nothing to prevent him from doing so.'

'On your own admission your are entirely responsible for his death.'

'But not for his murder, nor can I be charged with manslaughter. Under English law, since I was under no special relationship to him, I was not bound to save him from accidentally killing himself. A man who passes a pond in which a child is drowning is under no legal obligation to try to save that child. A man seeing another about to shoot himself is not legally bound to do anything to stop him.'

Chapter Fifteen

AFTER HOLTER had finished giving his testimony, Adems spoke at length to his instructing solicitor and then stood up.

'Your evidence is at complete variance with the facts of the case.'

'Is that in the nature of a question or a comment?' asked Holter blandly.

'Have you listened to any of the evidence of other witnesses?'

'Naturally. I had to make certain it was correct.'

'Then do you seriously expect the jury to believe that what you've just told the court bears the slightest relationship to the truth?'

'Why shouldn't they?'

'Why shouldn't they? Can you reasonably ask that question?'

'Very reasonably.'

'How do you explain the absence of powder stains on the hands of the dead man since you claim it was he who fired the revolver?'

'The evidence was that there would not necessarily be any stains on the hand that fired the gun.'

'The evidence was that normally there are such stains, that normally they can be shown to exist, and that because there was none on the deceased's hand the expert witness was of the decided opinion that the deceased had not fired a gun that day.'

'This was obviously abnormal.'

'That is your only answer?'

'No, it isn't, as a matter of fact.'

'Very well, then, what other abnormal answer have you?'

'Well, you see, because Corry was fooling around, jeering at me, making me suffer the knowledge of my own impotence, he played the fool from beginning to end. Instead of holding the gun normally, he held it back to front with his thumb through the trigger guard. If you try that you'll see there wouldn't be any stains on the hand.'

'You're asking the jury to believe he held the revolver in that position?'

'Only because he was acting the fool.'

'Far too foolishly for anyone to believe in it.'

'I'm sorry, but that's what happened.'

'Why should he have believed the gun to be empty?'

'As you pointed out earlier in this trial, it was a natural

assumption to make. Didn't you say in your opening address that a casual murderer would surely have believed it to be empty because it was so openly displayed?'

'Never mind what I said,' snapped Adems, unwisely giving way to anger. 'Why should a man, found with your wife, suddenly start acting like a clown?'

'He very soon discovered he didn't have to fear me in a physical sense, then I suppose there was just enough decency left in him to be embarrassed.'

'If there was an initial scuffle, no matter how ignominious your part, why was there no bruising on the dead man's body? Doctor Kinnet testified that there was none, yet had there been the slightest scuffle he would have expected to find bruising.'

'I'm afraid my attempts were just as ignominious as you've suggested. He fended me off with one jab from his right hand and although it bruised me, it can't possibly have bruised his hand.'

'And you made no further attempt to hit him?'

'I knew it wouldn't be any use. There wasn't anything I could do.'

'Except shoot him.'

'He shot himself by accident.'

Adems tipped up the seat on his immediate right and stepped into the space he had just created. 'If all that you say is true, why didn't you call in the police and explain what had happened as an innocent man would have done?'

'At all costs I wanted to keep my wife clear of everything. I knew what people would think if it came out that she and Corry had been together in chambers.'

'What would they think?'

'That she and Corry were having an affair.'

'But isn't that precisely what you've told this court?'

'My wife was sufficiently injudicious to have a mild flirtation with Corry. Obviously, she was very ill-advised, but she was never in any danger of committing adultery.'

'From what you heard outside that room in chambers, you must have thought they were lovers?'

'From what I heard when I was outside, I knew they were most definitely not.'

'Then it is nonsense to say you were mad with jealousy

when you burst into the room. You knew very well there was no need to be jealous.'

'I love my wife very much and the thought that she might have shared even a little of her affections with another man was enough to make me almost mad with rage.'

'Mad enough to want to kill him?'

'At the time of entering the room, yes.'

'If Corry were so much stronger and you knew it, why should he need a gun to defend himself?'

'But he wasn't trying to defend himself. He was trying to humiliate me.'

'Humiliate you? By shooting himself?'

'By pretending he would like to shoot himself to show how much more important I was than he, when it was so very obvious he didn't think this and wasn't going to shoot himself.'

'You're crediting him with the most ridiculous motives.'

'He was playing the part of a fool.'

'After he had cocked the gun and released the safety catch, which you claim he did, you knew that if he pulled the trigger he would shoot himself if the gun was aimed at him?'

'Yes.'

'You admit you hated him enough not to warn him?'

'At the time, yes.'

'Are you trying to say you didn't hate him a few seconds later?'

'He was dead then.'

'When, much later, you re-discovered the photograph of your wife in the drawer of your desk, why did you smuggle it out of the building?'

'Once again, to try to hide from the world the fact that my wife had been having this mild flirtation. The world is a malignant gossip.'

Adems looked down at his brief. He was a reasonably clever man, yet only now did he fully realize how Holter had waited until all the prosecution evidence had been given and then had brilliantly used that evidence to support his own story, as a judo expert uses his opponent's momentum to win the fall. The evidence had been proved by the prosecution and so could not be challenged by the prosecution. There *had* been a woman in the room, she *had* been Charlotte Holter, she *was* dressed in a strawberry pink dress, it *was* her compact which had fallen to the ground and spilled some of her face-powder on to the carpet, Holter *had* arrived at The Three Bells late and in a state ...

'Yes?' said the judge harshly.

* * *

The verdict was delivered at a quarter to seven in the evening and when it was given the judge began to speak angrily, but checked himself so quickly that no one was certain what he had been going to say.

The court slowly emptied. Accepting the suggestion of an usher, Holter and Charlotte left the building by a side entrance in order to escape any crowd or newspapermen who might be waiting. They walked, unnoticed, along the street to the car park in which was Charlotte's Mercedes.

As they reached the first set of traffic lights, at red, Charlotte braked the car to a halt. Holter lit a cigarette. He suddenly laughed loudly. 'By God, old Proctor's expression was one to remember. He'd have pulled the lever of the trap door himself given half the chance.'

The lights changed and she released the handbrake and drove on.

'It must have been a terrible time for you,' he said. 'Worrying yourself sick about me. You were wonderful in court, Betty, absolutely wonderful. Damn it, you had me nearly believing you were in the room when Corry was shot.'

'Stop it.'

'No, but it's true, darling. What an actress. Even the way you showed yourself to be under a mental strain was just right.' He laughed again. 'Adems must be wondering what hit him.'

'Someone shot Corry.'

'And as I've always said, it wasn't anyone from chambers. That's unthinkable. The brotherhood of the Bar means far too much.' He began to whistle, out of tune. He thought that there couldn't be as many men as he had fingers on his right hand who could have carved a way through the prosecution's case as he had.

'What's going to happen?' she asked, her voice high.

'In what way?'

'Will the police go on looking?'

'I suppose so. Maybe this time they'll look in the right places. Any man with any sense of what's right and what's wrong would know it wasn't one of us.' He was silent for a while and when he did speak again there was an unusual note in his voice. 'This case has really shocked me, Betty. I was completely innocent and yet I was close to being found guilty. And that in an English court of law. Of course, it wasn't the law's fault, it was the evidence. What can you do when a witness like that Wallace makes so gross a mistaken identification? He probably saw some local tart, yet he convinced himself he saw you. Damn' well makes one remember Adolph Beck.'

'Who?'

'Beck. He was convicted of a crime he had nothing to do with and served a seven year jail sentence. Nearly happened to him a second time, what's more. Something ought to be done about eye-witness identification. . . .'

'Stop talking about it.'

'All right.' He lowered the window and flicked his cigarette out on to the road. Fields were beginning to take the place of houses and he stared at them with a vague, undefined feeling that they were the first real proof of his freedom. The harvest, an early one, was over and stretches of stubble alternated with straw-coloured grass which offered visible evidence of the dryness of the summer.

They turned off the main road and reached Crighton. Two women, with prams, were gossiping outside the butchers and as the car slowed down they looked at it. One of them obviously recognized him because she suddenly gasped. He chuckled. In next to no time the news would be around that he was free and back in the big house. He knew that the villagers would be glad.

She garaged the car and they walked round the side of the house and entered through the front door, beneath the massive porch.

'There's nothing for supper,' she said in a lifeless voice as he closed the door.

'Not expecting me home, darling? Don't say you'd already ordered the sackcloth and ashes?' He kissed her without noticing her lack of response. 'I'll go down to the cellars and get some champagne to celebrate.'

He drank most of the champagne. At the meal, she ate little of the food.

'Have a brandy?' he said, once they were back in the sitting-room.

'I don't want anything.'

'Betty, my darling, stop worrying. It's all over and done with. Try to forget I was ever in danger.'

'How can I forget anything when you keep on and on about it?'

He looked quickly at her and then away. He crossed the room and poured himself out a very generous brandy. She had these moods and when she was in one it was a long time before she could escape it. She had naturally been very shocked by his arrest and trial and had plainly expected him to be found guilty. Now that he was innocent and back at home, it was going to take her time to readjust her ideas.

He sat down, warmed the glass in the palms of his hands, and drank.

'I'm tired,' she said suddenly. 'I'm going to bed.'

'All right, darling. I shan't be long.'

She stood up, hesitated, and came across to him. She sat down on the arm of his chair. 'I'm sorry I keep snapping at you, Radwick, but I feel in such a muddle.'

'Of course you do.'

'I expect I'll soon be better.'

'How about going abroad for a holiday as soon as we can? Would that be fun?'

'Anywhere with you is fun.' She kissed his cheek and stood up.

He watched her leave the room. Once more, it came to him how impossible it was to think of her age in terms of being half his. She was young and vibrantly alive, but between them there was no suggestion of the mental gap that was supposed to exist between people of disparate ages.

He and she thought alike, lived alike, and loved alike. He finished his brandy, had another and smaller one, and went upstairs.

When he entered their bedroom, Charlotte was stripped to the waist.

He shut the door. 'God, you're beautiful!' His voice was suddenly hoarse.

She turned and faced him. 'Am I, Radwick? Do you really mean that? You know, I try to be beautiful for you.' She came forward and took hold of his hands in hers. 'Darling, you never really doubted me, did you?'

'You know I didn't.'

'When you asked me to say I'd been in that room, I was terrified you'd begun to think it was the truth?'

'You're so silly.' He drew her to himself and began to slide his hands down her smooth flesh. Now it was he who no longer wanted to discuss the case.

Chapter Sixteen

TRAYNTON LOOKED up from his desk. 'Good morning, sir,' he said, as Holter came into the clerks' room.

' 'Morning, Josephus. How's life been?'

'Very, very sad, sir. I have had to return at least two thousand guineas. One brief from London was marked at five hundred.'

'When was that for?'

'Next week, sir.'

'Then why did you return it?'

'The circumstances being what they most unfortunately were, sir, I felt quite unable to guarantee you being able to conduct the case.'

'I should have thought you'd have had more faith in me than that.'

'However faithful, sir, I had to observe the etiquette.'

'To hell with etiquette. Your trouble is, you're just a professional pessimist.'

'I do no more than work to my best judgment, sir,' replied Traynton, deeply hurt.

Holter crossed to the mantelpiece and looked down at the briefs. When he next spoke, his voice was grave. 'What's the verdict going to be, Josephus? Will they keep on briefing me?'

'The view has been expressed to me, sir, and I venture to quote the exact words, that if you were such a cunning old bastard as to get yourself off that clear a murder charge, you were the cleverest counsel at the Bar and worth briefing if you'd murdered half a dozen Corrys.'

'This person didn't doubt I was guilty, then?'

'I've no idea, sir.'

'I suppose I shouldn't go around asking that question?'

Resse came into the clerks' room and he was closely followed by Marriott, who was carrying some books.

''Morning, Radwick,' said Resse. 'Is it in order to congratulate you?'

'I wouldn't know,' replied Holter, defensively.

'They tell me Proctor has had some kind of seizure and keeps on muttering that Dickens was quite right.'

'Good morning, sir,' said Marriott. 'I'm very pleased to see you back.'

'Very heartfelt words,' jeered Resse. 'He couldn't think of anything but all the shillings in the pounds he was in danger of losing.'

The telephone rang and Traynton answered it. Without any sense of transition, Holter was swept back into the life of chambers and it was as if there had never been a break.

He went to his room. As he sat down at his desk, he noticed the bare top. Was Traynton right when he said the briefs would keep coming? Solicitors were notably conventional and rarely briefed counsel whose name had been touched by scandal. Was it scandalous to have been charged with a crime someone else committed?

Traynton stepped just inside the room. 'You're leading at Canterbury next Monday, sir. And there's another set of papers coming in for an opinion.'

When alone, Holter leaned back in his chair. The wings of poverty had almost touched him, but now they were flying away. A counsel without briefs was a man without a career: trouble could reduce an income from thousands to hundreds, or even tens, in less time than it took to realize the fact. He could have withstood many things, but never poverty. His life had to be the life of a large and luxurious home, good food and drink, lavish entertainment, expensive holidays abroad, and the ability to give Charlotte whatever she wanted.

The door opened and Traynton came into the room once more. He shut the door.

'Well?' said Holter. 'What's the latest? A thousand clinking golden guineas for my services?'

'No, sir.'

Holter noticed Traynton's expression. 'What?'

'The Under Treasurer of your Inn has just been in telephonic communication with me, sir.'

'What about?'

'There's to be a hearing before the Benchers on Friday next week, sir.'

'I'm being charged?'

'I fear so, sir, with conduct unbecoming a barrister and a gentleman. The Under Treasurer said that the Benchers wish to inquire into your conduct and the means you employed in your defence and to judge whether they were such that a Queen's Counsel should have employed them, or not.'

'Goddamn it, did they expect me to fight with kid gloves on?'

'I fear, sir, that it may be alleged that you have tended to bring discredit upon the profession.'

Holter stood up and crossed to the window. Barristers guarded the reputation of their profession with the fierce jealousy of a mother guarding her daughter's virginity. The controlling body of each Inn of Court was the Benchers: ironically, he was a Bencher of his Inn. Now, he was to be tried in the case of the murdered Corry for the second time. *Nemo debet bis vexari, si constat curiae quod sit pro una et eadem causa*, but if the cause was the same, the form was not. He had been found not guilty of murdering Corry.

Now, he was to be tried for the means he had used to escape conviction and because he had admitted in court to moral responsibility for Corry's death.

He almost shouted when he next spoke. 'Did they expect me to worry about being a gentleman rather than clearing myself of a murder charge? Aren't I allowed to be as energetic in my own defence as in defence of anyone else?'

'Caesar's wife, sir.'

'Neither he nor his wife was above suspicion. What did you expect me to do?'

'I'd rather not answer, sir.'

'Why not?'

'My position, sir.'

Holter returned to his desk and rested his hands on the top of it. 'You'd rather I'd abided by the rules, wouldn't you, even if that meant I was found guilty of a murder I didn't commit? Admiral Sahib going down with the ship in full dress uniform.'

'So many things have changed over the years, sir, and I am too old to understand them.'

Holter sat down. The wings of poverty were back, beating more strongly than ever. The jealous Benchers had the right to disbar him and that meant his income would drop to nothing.

'Sir,' said Traynton, 'I shall be retiring that Friday. Would it be in order for Marriott to accompany you to London for this hearing?'

'You don't want to end your connection with the law with my public disgrace?'

Traynton turned and, walking as though he were a very old man, left the room.

After the clerk had gone, Holter reached down to the bottom left-hand drawer and pulled it open. Inside was a half-bottle of whisky and two glasses. He poured himself out a strong drink.

How was he going to defend himself? How was he going to convince the Benchers, ready to be sanctimoniously shocked, that although innocent he had had falsely to admit to being morally responsible for Corry's death in order to escape actual responsibility for it? His troubled thoughts were interrupted by Marriott, who came into the room.

'Sorry to bother you, sir, but Detective Inspector Brock would like to see you.'

Holter shrugged his shoulders. 'All right.'

'I'm terribly sorry about the hearing in London, sir, but I know everything will be OK.'

'I hope you're right, George. Josephus doesn't want to come to London with me as it's his last day in chambers, so you'll have to.'

'Very good, sir.'

'I'll have to work out my defence. Ironic, isn't it? Having to defend myself against proving my own innocence!' When next he spoke, he did so far more briskly. 'All right, let's see the detective.'

Marriott went out and several seconds later Brock, carrying two small paper parcels, came in. 'Good morning, Mr Holter,' he said, in a flat voice.

'What's it this time?'

'I'm returning your property, sir.' Brock made it clear that because it was an unwelcome duty he had undertaken it himself.

'Property?'

'A photograph of your wife and a revolver.'

'Sit down and have a drink?'

'No, thanks.'

'You're still very certain, then?'

'Of some things.'

Holter poured himself another whisky. He lifted his glass. 'Here's to crime.'

Brock put the two parcels on the desk.

'My wife was never near here that Tuesday,' said Holter.

'No, sir.'

'And neither was I, not after I had left with Corry. For God's sake, man, with that evidence against me, what chance did I have?'

'A very good chance, it seems.'

'The murderer was a casual thief. Corry came back later because he'd left something behind and whilst he was inside he surprised the thief, who shot him.'

'You'd locked both doors.'

'The thief picked the locks.'
'The locks weren't picked.'
'You could have made a mistake.'
'Could I?'
'You're not infallible.'
'No, I'm not. Will you please check the revolver and photograph, sir, and make certain they're in order.'
'I'll take your word for it.'
'Have you a licence for the revolver?'
'No. Are you going to charge me?'
'I suggest you apply for one. There are no cartridges in the chambers.'
'Very well.'
'I would advise you to keep that cabinet locked in future.'
'I'll remember your recommendations.'

Brock left the room. He slammed the door shut behind himself.

Holter poured himself out a third whisky.

* * *

On the following Monday morning, after a week-end during which he had worked at his own defence, Holter rang the central police station as soon as he arrived in chambers. He asked for Detective Inspector Brock.

'Brock,' said Holter, 'I want your help.'

'I doubt there's anything I can do,' replied the other coldly.

'You owe me something.'

'Do I?'

'You saw to it I was charged with murder.'

'I did no more than hand the evidence to others.'

'Maybe, but let's not argue the point. I've got to appear before a hearing in London in connection with the trial. I want you to appear, if you will, and testify to the strength of the evidence against me.'

'You'll have to speak to the chief constable. If he tells me to attend, I will.'

'I'll speak to him. I'll pick you up in my car and we'll go to London by train.'

After he had replaced the telephone receiver, Holter stared out of the window. Brock did not bother to hide his feelings in the matter and such feelings were likely to be echoed in the Bencher's minds. If they were convinced of his guilt, a guilt he had escaped from solely by admitting to moral responsibility for the death, they would use his moral turpitude as the excuse for their punishment by disbarment of his guilt.

Chapter Seventeen

CHARLOTTE, ON the Friday, went with her husband to the garage. He swung one of the counterbalanced doors up and was about to go inside when she stopped him by putting her hand on his elbow.

'Good luck, my darling,' she said.

'I'll need all that's going.'

'Don't dare to start being pessimistic. I know you'll be quite all right because you're so clever.' She kissed him. 'You don't seem to realize what a brilliant husband I've got.'

He was not a fanciful man, but as he drove very rapidly towards Hertonhurst he wondered whether this would be one of the last times he would enjoy driving a Bentley? Suppose he had to sell it, and everything else, how much capital could he find? Two thousand for the Bentley, fifteen hundred for the Mercedes, fifteen thousand for the house and two thousand for the furniture, etc., and perhaps another three or four thousand from other sources, including her jewellery. In these circumstances, most people would have said it was utterly ridiculous to talk about the wings of poverty since he and Charlotte were clearly never going to starve, but to him it would be poverty because it would be failure. He would no longer be able to buy her jewellery or clothes specially designed for her, he would no longer be able to give her whatever she wanted.

As he entered the town, he drove across lights that had turned to red and narrowly missed a mini-bus. He cursed the other driver. Then he cursed the fools who never named roads so that drivers could tell where they were. It was only when he saw Marriott standing on the pavement that he realized he had reached the right place.

With Marriott to act as navigator, Holter was able to find Brock and Wallace within ten minutes. He drove from Hertonhurst to Ashford at speeds of up to eighty.

* * *

The Inn of Court had been built when Elizabethan architecture was flowering most luxuriously and the intricately carved hammer-beams in the roof were as magnificent as any in the country. At the north end of the rectangular hall was the dais on which the Benchers dined and at the south end was the gallery and underneath this the carved screen which was reputed to have been made from the wood of shipwrecked ships of the Spanish Armada. On the panelled walls there hung the armorial shields of past Treasurers.

Tables and benches had been pushed against the walls, leaving only two in the centre which faced the dais. The robing-room attendant, acting as usher, led Holter and the others across to these two tables. Holter sat down and motioned to Marriott to give him his brief-case. Although he refused to admit it to himself, he was more nervous now than he had been when on trial for the murder of Corry.

The door at the back of the dais was opened by the butler, in his brown fur-lined robes, and seven men, each of whom was wearing black coat and striped trousers, came on to the dais. Holter, as he stood up, recognized three high court judges and four QCs. With very heavy irony, he thought that justice in the courts must also have been brought to a stop so that he could be tried, a man who had been found not guilty by his own peers.

The Benchers sat down with the Treasurer, in the centre chair. He had a long, narrow face in which every line suggested autocratic authority, fostered over the years in which he had been a judge.

'Mr Holter,' said the Treasurer, 'you have been asked to

attend this hearing in order that we may decide whether your recent conduct has been contrary to that standard which is expected from a member of the Bar.'

'Yes, sir,' said Holter.

'You have recently been tried at Brackensham Assizes on a charge of murder. The verdict was "not guilty." You are reported as having made the following admissions at the trial: that you were present in the room with Corry, the deceased, that he picked up a revolver which he believed to be empty but you knew to be loaded, that he jokingly threatened to shoot himself, and that you made no effort to inform him of the true condition of the gun – indeed, you carefully explained how the gun could be fired – so that when he pulled the trigger he shot and killed himself. Did you make these admissions?'

'Yes, sir.'

'Very well. Are you proposing to ask this hearing to allow you to call witnesses in support of your case?'

'I am, sir. I should like to call Detective Inspector Brock and Mr Edward Wallace.'

The Treasurer turned and spoke to the three men on his right and to the three on his left. He addressed Holter again. 'We feel that it will be best if your witnesses retire from Hall until you wish to call them. With their permission, they will be escorted to the Benchers' Common Room.'

The butler came down from the dais to the centre of the hall and escorted Brock and Wallace up on to the dais, past the end of the long table, and out of Hall through the rear doorway.

'Mr Holter,' said the Treasurer, 'I shall state briefly the reasons for holding this hearing and then you may make whatever statement you wish and may call your witnesses. Any member of this tribunal is at liberty at any stage of the proceedings to ask whatever questions he may wish. Afterwards, we shall retire. We hope to be able to give you our decision today. If we feel unable to do this, we shall deliver it to you at the first opportunity.

'Mr Holter, in the full knowledge of the fact that you are a Bencher of this ancient and honourable Inn, and have been for the past eight years, it must be presumed that you are fully aware of the ethical and moral standards required of all counsel who practise at the English Bar. These standards are not light ones and in many cases may fairly be said to be far higher than are normally to be found in modern society and counsel is required to act with greater moral honesty than is demanded by law. Such standards are, like the British Constitution, largely unwritten: no man can turn over the pages of a text book and find them all, although some of them have been listed.

'Counsel is required to conduct himself with honour in court, by which is meant honour to himself, his client, and the court. An assurance from counsel is accepted by the court: he has spoken on his honour and his honour will not be questioned.

'Because counsel has to be a man of honour and be seen to be a man of honour, he must do nothing which contradicts such state. Certain things obviously present such contradiction: if counsel is found guilty of fraud, *exempli gratia* clearly he is no longer a man of honour.

'We, the Benchers of this ancient and honourable Inn, feel that your actions and admissions in a properly constituted court of law were such that they must be closely examined by us. We desire to know whether you can justify yourself for having been responsible for the death of a man who accidentally killed himself when one word from you would have prevented his death. We are aware, as anomalous as this may be, that without a specific duty owing to a person there is no legal obligation to do anything to save his life, but we are concerned here with the question as to whether a moral obligation existed and whether you did, in fact, not meet that obligation.

'Will you please address this hearing, Mr Holter.'

Holter rearranged his papers on the table and in doing so knocked his pencil to the floor. Marriott picked it up. Holter cursed himself for being under so strong a state of nervous tension. 'Sir,' he said, 'I would submit that there is no case for me to answer.'

'On what grounds?'

'At the time in question I was not prosecuting or defending counsel, I was the accused. In such circumstances, I cannot be said to be bound by the rules of professional conduct.'

'Unless or until counsel is disbarred, Mr Holter, he is a counsel in the eyes of both the law and the public.'

'Very well, sir. Then I have either to defend myself as a man who told the truth in court and so may be held to be morally responsible for another man's death, or as a man who lied on oath to escape conviction for a crime he did not commit.'

'Or to escape conviction for a crime he did commit.'

'Sir, this hearing is, by the verdict of a jury, bound to accept the fact of my legal innocence.'

'That finding was in a criminal court. This is not a criminal court of law and is therefore not bound by such previous verdict.'

'But not to accept it is to say that this tribunal reserves the right to re-try me. It may have the right, but such right can only be equitable if all evidence previously given in court is again available to be called here.'

The Treasurer conferred with his fellow Benchers. 'We feel the point is well taken.'

'Sir, as an innocent person accused of murder, I was faced at the trial by a weight of evidence against me so great that only the most exceptional action on my part could have had any hope of gaining for me the correct verdict of not guilty. To have restricted myself to the normal limits of evidence would have been to ensure my conviction.'

'It will be difficult to convince us of that.'

'That is why I am calling two witnesses. Detective Inspector Brock was in charge of the police investigations and Edward Wallace made a very vital identification.'

'Very well.'

'I should first like to call Detective Inspector Brock.'

The butler left the Hall and returned in less than half a minute with Brock, who was led to the second table before the dais.

The Treasurer spoke to Brock. 'Inspector, you are not on oath, but this hearing expects you to speak the truth.'

'Yes, my lord.'

'Mr Holter will ask you certain questions and then either I or my fellow Benchers may require you to be more explicit on any of the points that have been raised.'

Carefully and slowly, Holter led Brock through a broad description of the police investigations and how he had come to the conclusion that Charlotte Holter had been present in chambers, that Holter had surprised her and Corry, that he had shot Corry and dragged the body across the floor to deposit it under the photograph of his wife.

'Inspector,' said the Treasurer, 'would you have considered the case against Mr Holter an overwhelming one?'

'Yes, my lord. When it became certain Mrs Holter was present I became convinced that this was a murder by a jealous husband.'

'I understand that despite all the evidence actually given in court, Mr Holter in fact strongly denies his wife was present?'

'That is so, my lord.'

'I think the point is this,' said one of the other Benchers. 'You were convinced Mrs Holter was present and if this were so then all the other evidence fell into line with the certainty that her husband was the murderer?'

'Yes, my lord.'

The Treasurer spoke. 'Would you agree with what Mr Holter said earlier, that if he was an innocent man he was in such dire risk of being found guilty only exceptional action on his part could possibly hope to bring about a verdict of not guilty?'

'At the beginning of the trial I was certain he would be found guilty.'

'Do you consider that an innocent man who finds himself in danger of being pronounced guilty of a crime is entitled to use any means whatsoever to escape conviction?'

'If he's innocent, yes.'

'Thank you, Inspector.' The Treasurer spoke to Holter. 'Do you wish to put any further questions to the witness?'

'No, thank you, sir. I should like to call Mr Wallace.'

Brock left the table he had been standing at, crossed to Holter's table and sat down beyond Marriott. Wallace was escorted into Hall by the butler.

After the Treasurer's warning about speaking the truth although not on oath, Holter began to question Wallace.

'I want you to give your evidence now as clearly as you

gave it at the trial. The preliminary facts are, are they not, that you work in Hertonhurst, on the evening of the Tuesday you had been to see a sick relative, and that on your way home you walked along the High Street, past the building in which are the chambers?'

'Yes, that's right.' Wallace was not nearly as self-assured in manner as he had been at the trial, almost as if the sense of history which permeated the medieval hall had overawed him.

'What time was this?'

'A quarter to seven. The church clock was striking so there wasn't no argument.'

'Will you please tell the hearing what you saw?'

'A woman comes out of the building. She comes hurrying out on to the pavement and past me.'

'Did you see her face?'

'No, not properly.'

'Was there a reason for this?'

'I wasn't really looking at her face, like.'

'Why not?'

'The dress she had on was one of them with the kind of plunge what looks as if it's going to reach the ground.'

'Was the plunge in the shape of a V?'

'That's right.'

'Do you remember what the dress was like?'

'Well, it was pink, a strawberry pink, and it couldn't have been a tighter fit, not if she'd been poured into it. There wasn't no belt. The buttons was the same pink as the dress.'

'What colour was this woman's hair?'

'Blonde, real blonde. It got me started on thinking about strawberries and cream.'

'Did you notice anything else?'

'Her shoes and her handbag was the same colour as her dress.'

'Can you remember what kind of collar the dress had?'

'No.'

Holter faced the Benchers. 'Sir, the relevance of this evidence lies in the fact that my wife has her dresses designed by Miss West. Miss West testified in court that on the Tuesday, when my wife left Miss West's house, she was wearing a dress which exactly matches this description and that since it had been designed by Miss West it was almost certainly unique. It will be very obvious, sir, that on the face of it, this evidence proves quite conclusively that the woman who came out of chambers at a quarter to seven was my wife. But since I knew that it was not my wife, it was very clear to me at the trial that here was a coincidence of truly staggering proportions, so staggering that it was almost impossible for any juryman to believe it was a coincidence. If the jury accepted all the other evidence and then believed this witness, Wallace...'

'I was telling the truth,' said Wallace loudly.

Holter unsuccessfully tried to hide his annoyance at the interruption. 'I was not suggesting you were lying. I was merely pointing out that if, quite reasonably, the jury accepted all your evidence, they must ignore the possibility of a coincidence and must believe this woman to have been my wife. Your evidence...'

'She was dressed like what I said.'

'No one denies that.'

'I can still see the dress in me mind.'

The Treasurer spoke impatiently. 'No one is suggesting that you can't.'

'It had this plunging neckline, and two pleats, and there weren't no belt, and the shoes and handbag was the same colour, and there was a bit of sticking plaster on her ankle...'

'What?' shouted Holter.

Wallace stared at him.

'What did you say?'

'I only said there was this bit of sticking plaster.'

'You've never mentioned that before.' Holter's face was white and his hands were trembling. 'You've just made that up.'

Brock, startled by the turn of the evidence, suddenly lost all his hatred for the other and felt only a bitter sadness.

Wallace was frightened by the effect of his words. 'I didn't make nothing up. There was sticking plaster on her ankle.'

'Which ankle? Come on, man, which ankle?'

'Well, it was ...' Wallace's face was screwed up in an expression of concentration. 'It was the right one.'

'Whereabouts on the ankle?'

'On the outside: on the bit what sticks out. It wasn't very big, but I noticed it rucked up her stocking a bit.'

Holter sat down abruptly, as if his legs would no longer support him. He sat, motionless, his face showing the private hell of his utter misery.

There was a drawn-out silence. No one looked at Holter, except for Wallace who was too slow-witted to have realized yet what the new piece of evidence had meant to Holter.

'Thank you,' the Treasurer finally said.

'Have ... have I said something wrong?' Wallace blurted out.

'Please sit down.' The Treasurer waited until Wallace was sitting down before he spoke again: 'We shall retire now, to consider the evidence.'

The Benchers stood up and, with the Treasurer at their head, filed out of the hall, past the butler who held the door open for them.

Wallace came half-way across to the second table. He looked at Holter, then Marriott, then Brock. 'I ... I didn't mean ...'

'It can't be helped,' replied Brock wearily.

'But what's so special about the sticking plaster,'

'Let's leave it for the moment.'

'But I just don't get it.'

'I tell you what, Mr Wallace, it's going to be some time before anything happens so suppose you and Mr Marriott go out and get a drink?'

'Always willing to drink, I'm sure.'

Brock spoke to Marriott. 'I'll stay.'

Marriott said nothing, but stood up and left, followed by Wallace.

Brock watched them walk the length of the great hall, beneath the huge double arching beams, and go through one of the two doorways in the oak screen. He lit a cigarette. Holter could be called a fool for taking so long to recognize the truth, but he wasn't the first husband to be a fool and he wouldn't be the last. Brock drew on the cigarette. Holter had never believed it was his wife in chambers with Corry and so Holter wasn't the murderer.

'I ... I never doubted her,' said Holter. 'D'you understand, I never doubted her.'

'No, I know.'

'I believed her, whatever the evidence was. It didn't mean anything that Betty was with that West woman or had borrowed the car when her own seemed perfectly all right. The rest of the world could be bloody-minded enough to want to think she'd driven to chambers for some dirty assignation, but I knew she hadn't because she'd told me she hadn't. I believed Wallace had seen another woman with blonde hair and a pink dress. That sort of coincidence can happen. But there couldn't be two women with blonde hair, pink dresses, pink shoes, pink handbags, and both with bits of sticking plaster on the same part of the same ankle. That couldn't be a coincidence. Betty grazed her ankle in the kitchen that morning. It bled so I put on a plaster strip with some TCP ointment. Oh, God, it was Betty in chambers!'

Chapter Eighteen

THE BENCHERS returned to Hall and sat down. The Treasurer spoke to Holter.

'We are agreed that the circumstances in which you found yourself were so extraordinary that in our opinion you were justified in what you did, even though you used the law to defeat the law. We wish to add that only such quite exceptional circumstances warrant the action you took and that our acceptance of your actions sets no precedent. Counsel must be completely honest with any court and can never normally be justified in using their special knowledge of the law to defend themselves.'

The Benchers stood up and left the hall. Since they all knew Holter quite well, they were embarrassed by what had happened and were eager to escape from his presence.

Brock spoke. 'Let's go, Mr Holter.'

Holter forced himself to accept that no matter how great was his misery, the world had not stopped turning. 'All right.'

Brock collected up the papers on the table and carefully packed them into the brief-case. 'We've got to find Marriott and Wallace. Perhaps we can have a drink with them if they're still in a pub.'

'All right,' said Holter for the second time.

They left the hall, passing through the left-hand doorway in the screen. A man in white coat and striped trousers was waiting to lock up. 'How did it go, sir?' he asked.

'Mr Holter has not been disbarred,' replied Brock.

'Very glad to hear it, sir.' The attendant looked at Holter's misery-haunted face. 'Been a bit of a shock, like?'

'Yes,' agreed Brock, 'it has.'

*   *   *

Holter and Marriott arrived back at chambers at 5.20 in the afternoon. Holter went straight through to his room, brushing past Traynton who asked with pathetic eagerness what had happened, and sat down at his desk. The first thing he was really conscious of was the framed photograph of a smiling Charlotte. He picked it up and threw it on to the ground. The glass did not break because of the way it fell on to the carpet. Cursing, he leaned over, picked it up, and replaced it on the desk.

He lit a cigarette. Into his mind there flashed picture after picture of Betty and himself together: coming out of the registry office, their honeymoon on the luxury cruise, buying her clothes which were so expensive that for the first six months she was frightened to wear them, buying jewellery, Charlotte laughing, Charlotte wildly and passionately making love...

He stubbed out the cigarette in the ash-tray. When a woman did this to you, what was the answer? Kill her? God, how he wanted to because he knew that he never could, or would. 'Yet each man kills the thing he loves.'

There was a knock on the door and Marriott came in. 'About Mr Traynton's farewell party, sir? Shall I say you can't attend?'

He wanted to answer yes, but instinct told him that in carrying out his duty lay his only hope for temporary mental rest. 'I'm coming. Has anyone put the champagne on ice?'

'It's all in a tin bath I managed to borrow from the florists down the road, sir. Mr Resse saw to getting the ice from the fishmongers earlier on.'

'How many bottles?'

'The six, sir. If that's all finished, there won't be anyone going home this side of tomorrow.'

'What about the savouries?'

'All delivered. And I made very certain we got the proportion of caviar we ordered.'

'Does Josephus know what happened at the hearing?'

'I've not told him.'

He didn't know why, but it seemed to matter a great deal to him whether Traynton knew what Charlotte had done to him. 'Are Oliver and Alan ready?'

'Yes, sir, and Mr Aiden.'

Holter looked at his watch. 'Josephus will be putting on his outdoor clothes any minute now. We'd better start.'

'Have you got the pen and pencil?'

Holter pulled open the top right-hand drawer of his desk and took out the case on which, in gold, were Traynton's initials. He dropped the case into his coat pocket and stood up.

He walked into the clerks' room as Marriott went to call the other members. Traynton was still by his desk, aimlessly checking that everything was neat and tidy. He was plainly bewildered because it did not seem as if he was to be offered any official good-bye and that hurt after fifty-six years in the same chambers, for thirty-five of which he had been head clerk.

'If you don't hurry, Josephus,' said Holter, 'you'll be late away.'

Traynton produced his gold hunter from his waistcoat pocket and opened the front. 'I had no idea it was that late, sir.' His expression was one of pain borne with dignity.

Puffing slightly, he stepped clear of the desk. 'I must, indeed, depart.'

'We'll be very sorry to see you go.'

'The time of retirement, sir, comes to all of us and I must confess I am not in harmony with the world of today. My one regret, if I may be permitted the liberty, is that Marriott has not had quite as much experience as I would wish him to have had.'

'He'll learn.'

'I trust your prognosis is not too optimistic, sir.' Traynton sighed deeply, went across to the stand, and picked up his umbrella, machintosh, and bowler hat.

At that moment the door opened and all the other members of chambers came in and Traynton realized that he was not after all to go without some recognition of this unique event. He became bashful and tried to make out that he had no idea what was about to happen.

They crowded round in a rough semi-circle in the centre of which stood Traynton, with bowler hat in one hand, mackintosh and umbrella in the other.

'We want to try to thank you for all you've done for us,' said Holter.

'For some of us, anyway,' murmured Resse, but not very loudly.

Holter continued. 'A chambers is only as good as its chief clerk and these chambers are first class. There isn't one of us here who doesn't owe you everything and to mark just a small fraction of our very deep appreciation for all you've done for us we'd like to give you a small present by which we hope you'll remember us for many, many years to come.' Holter handed the case to Traynton.

Traynton fingered the case, tracing out his initials. He opened it and stared at the matching gold pen and pencil, picked up the pen and held it in his right hand. 'It's ... it's wonderful, sir,' he said brokenly.

Good-bye Mr Chips, thought Resse, almost angry because the scene was affecting him as much as it was.

At a sign from Holter, Marriott left the room. Traynton tried to make a speech of thanks, but choked over the words. Spender started singing 'For he's a jolly good fellow' to ease the sense of nostalgia.

Traynton sat down at his desk and took out a sheet of paper from the top drawer. Carefully, he wrote first with the pen and then with the pencil. 'They're wonderful, really wonderful,' he said, as if they were the first he had ever seen.

Marriott came back with a tray on which were six glasses and two bottles of champagne. He filled the glasses and handed them around.

Holter raised his glass. 'I give you Josephus Traynton, our friend.'

They drank. Marriott brought in the savouries on two plates and Aiden ate as much caviar as he could, not deigning to move on to the smoked salmon until he had to.

By the time the third bottle of champagne had been finished the kindly reminiscences had begun. Traynton recalled his first day at work, as an office boy, when the clerks had worn frock coats, scratched away with quill pens, and the great names at the Bar were as much actors as lawyers.

During the drinking of the fourth bottle, Aiden discovered all the smoked salmon had been eaten and he loudly demanded to know who had swiped it all. Traynton said that back in the old days he had been noted for his dramatic delivery of a selected piece from *The Canterbury Tales*. His listeners, unable to ignore so blatant a hint, asked him to recite that same piece now. They had expected to hear a little of The Prologue, but were amazed when Traynton, between giggles, declaimed the touching scene between Nicholas and Absolon at the end of the Miller's Tale.

Aiden laughed so much that Resse had to slap him on the back to prevent his choking. 'Good God!' said Aiden, when he could finally speak, 'fancy Old Misery being as gloriously vulgar as that.'

Holter picked up his glass and drank it empty. He lit a cigarette and as he blew out the match there was a sudden streak of burning pain in his mouth. A second pain was followed by a third, which spread down to his throat.

'Anything wrong?' asked Resse, coming across from the fireplace.

'There's a bloody awful burning in my throat and mouth. For God's sake, give me some more champagne.'

Resse picked up an opened bottle, still a quarter full, and filled Holter's glass. 'What kind of burning pain?'

'It's like knives slicing.' Holter groaned. The sweat stood out on his face and forehead. Almost immediately, the pains increased in intensity and frequency. The whole of his abdomen became filled with them. It was as though an ice-cold hand with red-hot fingers were tearing his kidneys to pieces. With sudden urgency, he needed to go to the lavatory and Resse helped him to stagger out of the room and across the corridor. The state of micturition became worse. Someone asked him who his doctor was and he tried to answer, but could only mumble unintelligibly. He began to vomit. The world became a small circle inside which there existed only excruciating pain.

Chapter Nineteen

HOLTER, SITTING up in the hospital bed in a private room, ate a peach. The coolness of its juice soothed his throat and temporarily banished some of the pain that still remained. He used the remote control to switch on the TV, but when it came on there was only horse racing or golf. He switched it off and began to read a book, but the banal plot irritated him and after a few moments he dropped the book on to the bedside table.

He lay back. His stomach and throat still gave considerable pain at times, but it was remarkable how alive he felt now considering how close to death they said he had been. He lit a cigarette. If he had died, his last recorded memory would have been of Resse shouting to someone to telephone for a doctor. That would have been that and Radwick Holter would have ceased to exist. The call for the doctor would have been his epitaph.

What in the name of hell, he thought with sudden intense

irritation, had so nearly killed him? He had asked the nurses and they had fobbed him off with answers that would have done for a five-year-old. He had asked the two doctors who were attending him and they had replied in meaningless generalities. Had it been some kind of heart attack? Food poisoning?

A nurse came into the room and said his wife had been twice to the hospital that day to try to see him, but that until the doctors gave their permission he was allowed no visitors. She left, after a careful look round to make certain everything was in place.

He stubbed out his cigarette. What was he going to say to Betty? Did he release all the tortured bitterness that had been born at the hearing before the Benchers? Or was there just nothing to say?

An hour later, a doctor came into the room. Holter vaguely recognized him as someone he had met at a cocktail party.

'Hullo, Holter, how's it going?'

'I'm all right except for stabbing pains in my stomach and throat.'

'You'll get those for a while, I'm afraid, but looking ahead you should be OK before long.'

'What hit me?'

The doctor stared at him for several seconds before answering. 'Cantharidin poisoning.'

'Cantharidin?' The name was familiar. 'Is it some form of food poisoning?'

The doctor sat down on one of the two chairs. 'That depends on what kind of food you're in the habit of eating. Cantharidin is the active principle present in cantharides, a beetle. We use the stuff in hospitals, mainly as a diuretic. A lot of people in the outside world know it as Spanish Fly and are foolish enough to use it as an aphrodisiac.'

Holter could only stare blankly at the other.

'It's not the safest of things to deal with and there are a lot of doubts about its efficacy.'

'You ... you don't think I was talking it as an aphrodisiac?'

'Presumably you didn't imagine it was a pleasant afterdinner liqueur?'

'I didn't damn' well take it voluntarily. It was in my room in a phial along with a gun and knives and so on from my cases. Some of the stuff was given to a girl by a chap who wasn't making any headway. She died and he was up on a charge of murder.'

The doctor's expression changed. 'Did the revolver which killed Corry come from the same cabinet?'

'Yes.'

'You keep some pretty lethal mementoes.'

There was a short silence.

'Could it have been an accident?' asked the doctor.

'No.'

'I see. No wonder the detective's been around. He almost certainly saved your life.'

'Who? Brock?'

'That's his name. When you were brought in here you were well on the way to dying and we hadn't a clue what from. He came bursting into the hospital and said it was a thousand pounds to a penny the poison was Spanish Fly. After that, we were able to do something for you.'

Holter lit another cigarette. 'It's ... it's an odd thought that someone tried to kill me.'

'I'd call it a terrifying one.' The doctor stood up. 'Carry on as you are now and it won't be long before we can let you go home.' He chuckled. 'And don't rely on this stuff having any lasting impression!' He left.

Holter stared at the closed door and tried, and failed, to believe that he had been poisoned by someone outside chambers.

* * *

Brock visited him in the afternoon. He was carrying a paper bag which he held out. 'Hope you like grapes, Mr Holter?'

'Love 'em.'

Brock sat down. 'I saw your doctor outside and he says you're making very good progress.'

'Thank God. I hate the stink of hospitals.' Holter's voice became diffident. 'I hear you saved my life.'

'Maybe, maybe not. Someone here might easily have found out what it was you'd taken.'

'How did you know what was going on?'

'Mr Resse telephoned me from chambers and said you'd been carted off to hospital and it looked as if you'd been poisoned. I went round to chambers, remembered you telling me about the phial of Spanish Fly in the cabinet, made certain the phial was missing and rushed to this hospital to tell them.'

Holter began to eat some grapes. 'Do you ... Do you know who did it?'

'Yes, sir.'

'Who?'

Brock did not answer directly. 'I thought at first you might have been trying suicide because of what you'd learned up in London, but then I reckoned you were too much of a fighter for that. So I checked who in chambers knew about what had happened in London. They knew you'd been cleared, but nothing more.'

'Well?'

'They'd no idea you'd discovered the truth about your wife.'

'I wasn't bloody well going to broadcast the fact,' muttered Holter.

'Of course you weren't, but it was because you'd suddenly learned the truth that the attempt to murder you was made. The murderer was desperately afraid you'd now force your wife to tell the whole truth.'

To his intense annoyance, Holter discovered his brain was not working sufficiently clearly to understand the significance of what the other had said. 'If they didn't know, the poisoner didn't come from the chambers.'

'Unless one of them knew because he'd been at the hearing with you.'

'Marriott?'

'Yes, sir.'

'No. That's impossible. No.'

'He panicked because he was afraid. Because he panicked, he never stopped to realize that in murdering you he would be destroying the image of Corry as your wife's lover.'

'It can't have been Marriott.'

'He knew how you worshipped your wife and he was certain, quite rightly, you'd never disbelieve her. But he didn't know about the sticking plaster on her leg that Wallace would suddenly remember seeing.' Brock looked at Holter and thought, almost angrily, that no matter how egotistical a man might be, he could still be terribly hurt by another person.

'When did you know?'

'When you'd been poisoned.'

'What... what happened in chambers?'

'Your wife had been meeting Marriott there for some time. That Tuesday, they knew you would be safely away at the CA Harper Society dinner. Marriott left at his usual time and then returned after you and Corry had gone. He unlocked the doors with his keys and left them unlocked. Your wife, in a borrowed car in case the Mercedes was recognized, drove into town, parked the car, and walked to chambers. Just before she went into the building, Corry saw her.

'We'll never know why he was back there in the High Street, but it's easy to think up possible reasons. Anyway, he saw your wife go in and, with his perverted interest, wondered why because he could be certain she couldn't be expecting to meet you there. He waited a short while and then entered. He found the outer doors of chambers shut but not locked so he went in. If everything inside proved to be innocent, he could always produce a perfectly plausible excuse for his own presence.

'He listened outside your room long enough to become certain your wife and Marriott were ... and then he went in. He found them in ... in ...'

'In a compromising position,' said Holter harshly.

'Corry hated most people, for one bad reason or another. He hated your wife because she was young and beautiful and because she was deceiving you, just as his wife had deceived him years before. He jeered at her and asked her how you'd receive the news. He jeered at Marriott and wanted to know what kind of job Marriott thought his next one would be.

'Marriott, desperate because all the consequences were very clear, grabbed the gun out of the cupboard and threatened to kill Corry if he ever told anyone what had happened. Corry laughed and said that within twenty-four hours Marriott wouldn't be in a position to do anything to anybody. Corry naturally thought the gun was empty and Marriott's threats were even emptier. Marriott panicked and shot Corry.

'Your wife was naturally terrified. She tried to run out of the room, but tripped over her handbag which was on the floor. Her compact fell out and spilled powder on to the carpet.

'Marriott forced her to stay. He was shocked, but not so shocked he didn't try to save his own skin. He set the evidence to point at you. He knew that if you were tried, the prosecution couldn't call your wife.

'He dragged the body of Corry across the carpet and dumped it under the photograph of your wife. He knew how this would turn the police's minds to the Smith case.

'In retrospect, the trail of blood could have told us more than it did. In Smith's case, Smith found the woman had been deceiving him so he killed her and dragged her body to a photograph of himself: he was laying guilt before innocence. But Corry was laid before a photograph of your wife which would appear to be guilt being laid before guilt.

'Your wife, even in her shocked state, realized what Marriott was doing and tried to help you. She hid the photo in the bottom drawer of the desk. When it seemed certain you were the murderer, the hiding of this photograph merely seemed to point to an attempt on your part to conceal why you'd dragged the body to the desk. When it was certain you weren't the murderer, it became obvious that Corry wasn't the ... the lover. To attempt to incriminate you and then remove the final piece of incriminating evidence were two totally contradictory actions.'

'Was she trying to save me or her conscience?'

Brock was silent.

'She had to stand by her husband or her lover,' said Holter. 'So she stood by and watched me charged with murder. What happens now? Will she be charged as an accessory?'

'I don't know. You know more about the law than me.'

'More about the law and less about my wife.'

Brock stood up. Thankfully, he could now go.

*   *   *

The evening sunlight was coming through the window and casting a warm patch of light on the near wall when the sister came into Holter's room. 'Your wife's come to see you.'

'Tell her I'm too ill.'

'That's just being silly.' Not much more than half his age, she acted as if she were twice as old. 'You're not at all ill now. We'll just tidy things up a bit. There's this ... and this ... and put that there. Now, she can see you all neat and tidy.'

He tried to argue further, but she ignored him. Suddenly, a complete lethargy swept over him so that it seemed as if he could not have moved out of the bed if his life had depended on his doing so.

The nurse left and the pneumatically hinged door hissed shut. He stared at the patch of sunlight. In God's name, what did one say to a wife who had been prepared to see her husband convicted of murder rather than lose her lover?

The door opened and she came into the room. She was wearing one of Rachael West's dresses and looked very beautiful and very ... virginal. That word seemed to gain an independent life so that it could sit in his brain and jeer at him.

'Get out,' he croaked.

She came and stood by the bed.

'Get out, you lying bitch.'

She seemed to be crying. 'You must understand ...'

'He was my clerk. You had my clerk as a lover.'

She took hold of his right hand in both hers and he could not find the strength to free it. There was now a tear on each of her cheeks. 'I was terrified you were going to die, Radwick. I went to church and prayed. I hadn't done that since I was fifteen.'

'And how often did you pray for me when the police were hounding me? And how often did you pray for me during my trial?'

She sat down and forced his hand on to her lap.

'Why have you come here?' he demanded. 'Isn't he any more use to you now?'

'Radwick ...' She gulped. 'Radwick ...' She let go of his hand and took a handkerchief from her handbag.

'Was it more exciting with a guttersnipe of a clerk than with me? Was that it?'

'I promise you it wasn't like that, Radwick. Radwick, I swear I didn't know what I was doing. It wasn't me there, in chambers.'

'It wasn't anybody else's body he laid on.'

'I never began to love him.'

'You dirty whore.'

She put her hand to her mouth.

'Shocked you, have I? Did you reckon you could be my clerk's doormat without any complaints from me?'

'But I was mad. It wasn't me.'

'You knew who was who when I was charged with murder. You had to choose and you chose him.'

'I swear I didn't. Radwick, you're so cruel.'

'Cruel? What d'you call sleeping with my clerk?'

'Can't you see? I knew you'd never be convicted, Radwick. You're much too clever. I'd have told you the truth if there'd been any danger to you, but I desperately didn't want to hurt you.'

'You meant to carry on with him.'

'Won't you understand?'

'Not your bloody lying, no.'

'I don't want to leave you, Radwick. Ever.'

'Me, or my money?'

Before he had time to guess what she was going to do, she suddenly leaned across the bed and rested herself against him.

'Please, my darling, please, please understand,' she whispered.

Try as he did, he could not ignore the pressure of her breasts against his chest. He had a mental image of them, round, firm, cherry tipped, sweet, beautiful, responsive.

She ran the fingers of her right hand along the side of his face and then lightly brushed the lobe and inside of his ear. 'I so want to play ding-a-ling with you. Radwick, you don't really want me to leave you, do you? I know you're angry, but underneath you still love me, don't you? You still want me? D'you remember all the different fun things we were going to try? Could you live in that big house all on your own, sleeping in the bedroom and no one else in the bed with you? No one to kiss you, and love you? Could you stand being there and thinking of me with someone else?'

He groaned as his hands, of their own volition apparently, came round and began to caress her body.